"Play this when you get a chance. Thanks, Rafe. P.S. I'm flattered."

It appeared to be a video, though not a very clear one. There was no picture, only a dark smudge that looked like some kind of night shot, and the picture wasn't good at all, but the sound was exceedingly clear.

"Oh, yes...there...harder..."

The sultry voice filled the room, and Joy sat back in total shock. It sounded like *her*.

"You're so hard...I need you inside me...."

Realizing it *was* her, Joy sprang furiously into action, hitting the keyboard frantically and trying to shut the damned thing off—but somehow, due to the magic of computer technology and recalcitrant fingers, she turned up the volume even louder instead. The room was ringing with moans and sighs, and the sound ticked off a memory in her brain. Joy remembered the dream...and she knew what—and who—was coming next.

Blaze™

Dear Reader,

Happy holidays! It's that magical time again, when everything takes on an extra special glow. It's also the time of year when we all have added stress, pressures and conflicts—just like a good romance.

I wrote this book during spring in New York, and I set it in a Southern California heat wave—not exactly typical for a Christmas story. It was a blast writing a hot, sultry, Harlequin Blaze Christmas where the holiday spirit exists no matter the weather. Giving and receiving take on a sexy slant in *Talking in Your Sleep...*, but Rafe and Joy also learn about giving from the heart, and that the holidays are always best when spent with someone we love.

Thank you for giving me the wonderful gift of reading my book. I hope you'll drop me an e-mail at samhunter@samanthahunter.com or stop by my blog at www.loveisanexplodingcigar.com to share your own holiday thoughts and wishes!

Best wishes!

Samantha Hunter

SAMANTHA HUNTER
Talking in Your Sleep...

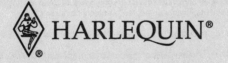

TORONTO • NEW YORK • LONDON
AMSTERDAM • PARIS • SYDNEY • HAMBURG
STOCKHOLM • ATHENS • TOKYO • MILAN • MADRID
PRAGUE • WARSAW • BUDAPEST • AUCKLAND

ISBN-13: 978-0-373-79369-3
ISBN-10:   0-373-79369-3

TALKING IN YOUR SLEEP...

www.eHarlequin.com

Printed in U.S.A.

ABOUT THE AUTHOR

Samantha Hunter lives in Syracuse, New York, where she writes romance full-time. When she's not plotting her next book, Sam likes to work in her garden, quilt, cook, read and spend time with her husband and their dogs. *Talking in Your Sleep...*, a steamy holiday story, marks her ninth Harlequin Blaze novel to date. Most days you can find Sam chatting on the Blaze boards at eHarlequin.com, or you can check out what's new, enter contests, or drop her a note at her Web site, www.samanthahunter.com, and at her blog, www.loveisanexplodingcigar.com.

Books by Samantha Hunter

HARLEQUIN BLAZE
142—VIRTUALLY PERFECT
173—ABOUT LAST NIGHT
224—FASCINATION*
229—FRICTION*
235—FLIRTATION*
267—HIDE & SEEK*
299—UNTOUCHED†
343—PICK ME UP**

*The HotWires
†Extreme
**Forbidden Fantasies

For all my readers, old and new,
thank you for your support, e-mails, cards, notes,
comments and kind thoughts. I wish you all the
happiest and most wonderful of holidays, that you
find your passions and that the magic of it
will stay with you all year long!

1

RAPHAEL MOORE TENSED his body then relaxed it one inch at a time. He began with his toes, moving up his calves to his knees, and concentrated on releasing the strain in his lower back. Breathing evenly, he imagined floating on a warm, soothing ocean current, the heat of the sun hypnotically beating down on him, and drifted off into a dreamy half consciousness that soon would lead to sleep.

"Oh, that's so good…. Touch me right there…."

"Dammit!" he cursed as his eyes shot open. The agitation of being wrenched out of his relaxed state doubled his shock. Taking a deep breath, he closed his eyes again, trying to control his heartbeat. He flexed his fingers in an attempt to catch hold of what had almost been his—a good night's sleep.

"I love how you kiss me. I want your mouth everywhere…."

He sat up, swinging his legs over the side of the bed, planting his palms tightly against his ears, attempting to block out the woman's voice. He could still hear her moans and sighs.

Obviously she was having a very good time, and he had no problem with that, but couldn't she do it with the window shut? He felt like some pervert, for Chrissakes, listening in.

The action happening a few yards away wasn't the only thing that was hot. A freak heat wave had temperatures up near ninety for Christmas in San Diego. It was inducing weird behaviors in everyone, the unusual weather combined with the usual holiday madness. His neighbors, however, seemed to enjoy being all sweaty.

After just having left the bitter cold of New York, he welcomed the heat, too. Summer was his favorite season. Even the smothering, humid city air in July and August didn't faze him. He'd happily embraced the West Coast, which didn't look at all Christmassy to him, in spite of the holiday decorations.

It felt like August, not December, and Rafe knew he'd made the right decision taking Warren up on his offer to stay here while his buddy was on his honeymoon in Thailand. Warren had grown up in the same Brooklyn neighborhood as Rafe. As kids they'd been inseparable and had served time on the volunteer ambulance together before Warren had decided that life wasn't for him. Now he had his own consulting business in sunny California. He'd been bugging Rafe to come out for a while, so Rafe had flown out for the wedding, then stayed to house-sit. It was great timing for both of them. Rafe had the place to himself for a month until Warren and his bride returned on January third.

If only for the neighbors, it would have been perfect. Warren had bought this little fixer-upper on a small residential street in North Park, and after the renovation the house was going to be fabulous. Rafe liked working with his hands, and it helped to have something to do. He was used to working, and he'd go nuts sitting around all day. He'd remodeled his entire apartment in Brooklyn, a relaxing activity in his off hours. Warren was happy to have him do some work on the house.

This was Rafe's first time in California, and he'd taken to it immediately. The sunshine and heat had lightened his mood as soon as he'd hit the tarmac. A native New Yorker, he hadn't been sure about leaving his home, but San Diego was heaven by comparison, at least at this time of year.

"A little lower...please...." a sexy woman's voice begged.

Rafe experienced a stirring in his groin that he had no business feeling, but hell, he was a man and he'd been listening to this monologue for three nights running. How many months had passed since a woman had talked to him like that? Insomnia was a libido killer.

Before his sleeplessness, his job had ruled his life, including his sex life. Being an emergency medical technician was all he'd ever wanted to do.

He'd thought about medical school, but he wasn't interested in the years of training it took to be a doctor. He liked the action of emergency services over being camped out in a classroom. Instead of spending the last twelve years studying how to help people, he'd been able to do it every day.

Despite the constant stress and pressure, for years he'd thrived on helping people when they needed it most. That was until this past year. Suddenly he couldn't sleep. Nothing helped, save the pills that he refused to take. Pills might address the insomnia issue, but they wouldn't solve the larger problem— why he'd burned out on the job after all those years, and why he couldn't handle it anymore.

All he could see was the endless stream of people in trouble and that they'd lost far too many of them. His last loss had been a five-year-old girl with asthma, alone at home in her tenement apartment. No one had been there to help her when she'd suffered a serious attack, and her parents hadn't been able to afford the costly medicines. Though the girl had been smart enough to dial 911, Rafe had gotten there too late.

Over the years, there had been so many cases like that he could barely keep count. Lots of good stories, too, but the bad ones were catching up with him. Like the husband and father of six children who had died right in front of him after being hit by a drunk driver, or the teenager shot on the street for no apparent reason while coming home from a graduation party. Their faces haunted Rafe as he lay awake in the dark hours of the night.

Something critical that had kept him sane seemed to have broken. The result was he'd lost his sense of purpose, his drive to do the work.

The insomnia might be a cause or a symptom, he still wasn't sure, but it had messed up his life for good. When he'd almost crashed the ambulance—with a patient on board—he'd been put on paid leave, and he couldn't argue with that decision. The company had taken his record into account and hadn't fired him— they were treating his break as accumulated sick and vacation time. However, if he couldn't solve his sleep problem, he knew he'd be in for permanent retirement.

The prospect made him feel hollow inside, and he pushed it away, knowing it would torture him for the rest of the night, at least. That was part of the problem, the endless thoughts that wouldn't stop, and the more he tried, the more they barged through, keeping him awake even when he was exhausted.

"Oh, yes…again…"

Rafe fell back on the bed, groaning, but not in pleasure. How long were they going to keep at it? It wasn't normal—these people went at it for hours every night. He wanted to be cool, to say, "More power to ya," but in truth he wanted them to shut the hell up and go to sleep.

Grabbing a pillow and heading to the sofa in the

living room, even though it was about eight inches too short for his six-foot frame, he walked out of the room, slamming the door behind him.

"DAD, I'M SORRY, I just can't—I know, it's yours and Lois's first Christmas together, so maybe it's better for you to spend it alone."

"Joy, we'd love to have you. It would be good for you and Lois to get to know each other."

Joy Clarke closed her eyes, exhausted, counting to twenty before responding. She'd met her new stepmother at her father's wedding, and liked her well enough. Lois was a nice woman who made her father happy. Still, Joy wasn't particularly interested in bonding. Her own mother had left them when she was nine. Since Lois was only ten years older than Joy, she was hardly a maternal figure.

"I know, that would be nice. Maybe in summer."

"That's what you said last spring."

"Work is crazy, Dad. I'm up for a promotion, and I can't afford to take time off now. Holidays are crazy in the toy business."

In truth, Christmas was a year-round holiday in her industry, everyone competing to get a jump on what the next hot product would be and making sure marketing and distribution was in place if they found it.

"I'm proud of what you've accomplished, Joy. You work hard, like I taught you, but I hope you'll be able to take some time off to come home. Perhaps once you get that promotion."

"Yeah, Dad. I have to go. Duty calls."

"Okay, sweetheart. Work hard, now."

"Always do," she said, hanging up the phone on the familiar exchange they'd shared since she was a child. He always told her to work hard—as he had—and she always did.

Joy settled her face in her hands, permitting herself a moment of quiet. She wanted a nap, badly. But a two-minute power-nap wasn't going to replace all the sleep she'd been losing thanks to restless dreams that were bothering her as much when she was awake as when she was asleep.

For several weeks, she'd had strange, muddled sexual dreams that left her edgy and restless. At first, they weren't about anyone in particular, just a shadowy figure who brought her to the edge of pleasure, but denied her real satisfaction. Then her neighbor, Warren, whom she barely knew, caught her by her car one day and told her a friend of his would be house-sitting over the holidays. She'd listened dutifully though honestly she had so much to do she didn't keep track of her neighbor's comings and goings. Warren told her the friend's name—Rafe Moore—and a general description. She hadn't thought twice about it at the time, until she'd seen the house sitter moving in, hauling his bags from the taxi that dropped him off.

Ever since...well, suffice to say her vague dream lover had taken on a real face. The experiences were getting much more intense, more explicit, and even more satisfying, but she woke up every morning exhausted. It was aggravating—why was she dreaming about this guy every night? She'd never even spoken to him, just watched him walk from the car to the house, puttering in the yard, in all his shirtless glory....

She groaned, trying to shake away the thoughts. It was bad enough he was in her head every night, let alone starting to obsess about him in the daylight hours. She had to work. She'd managed to dodge the bullet of having to go to her father's house for Christmas this year, using the one excuse her dad always gave merit: work. Never failed, but she wouldn't be able to put them off forever.

Her excuse was the truth though—she really was buried under work. The piles of papers and file folders stacked up all over her desk was proof of that.

As the public relations officer in charge of handling recalls, which happened fairly regularly in the toy-manufacturing industry, her responsibility was to make sure that the company's image didn't suffer when a product didn't work. God forbid anyone got hurt or worse, but sometimes it happened. Her whole life was about spin control, but she also legitimately tried to make sure that customers were taken care of, and would continue to buy Carr Toys.

She was good at doing that. Still, as corporate bottom lines became more pressing, manufacturing was forced to lay off more workers. The remaining staff had to pick up the slack, taking on more and more work. That had inevitably led to the making of more production mistakes. The result of those ended up in her lap. Her life had become a parade of broken toys and apologies on behalf of her company.

It wasn't what she'd pictured when she'd chosen PR as a major in college, where her classes had always been fun and exciting. Her professors had said she had talent, and she'd believed them. When she'd taken a job with a toy company, somehow she'd expected it to be fun. Six years later though, turning the corner of her thirtieth birthday, she knew better.

Carr was a multibillion-dollar company with three manufacturing locations, worldwide distributors and hefty competition within a troubled economy where customers were more than willing to sue when a product had a defect, especially a dangerous one.

Thanks to the triple punch of corporate downsizing, performance testing, and the replacement of older, more experienced employees with younger ones at lower pay and benefits, the work atmosphere had become increasingly cutthroat. She was up for a promotion, but she was also going against three other department managers who would be happy to sell their grandmothers for the same job.

Pressure, not fun, had become the name of the game. *Fun* was only a marketing strategy.

Joy could work under pressure because it was required of her, but it was something she'd had to become accustomed to. When things got tough, she remembered all the years her dad, who had been a utilities lineman, had worked weekends, holidays and whatever else he'd had to do to support them.

He never complained about it, and that taught her the value of hard work. She'd learned from his example. She took pride in what she did, but lately, in weak moments, she wondered if it was enough.

She straightened in her chair and turned her attention to the nearest pile of folders, picking the top one off and opening it. Then eyeing the calendar, she pursed her lips.

Two weeks before Christmas.

Joy felt no connection at all to the season, taking little part in the decorating, partying or shopping. Who had time? Her dad hadn't been much for Christmas after the year her mom left, and who could blame him? Joy had quickly learned that getting excited about Christmas was just setting herself up for disappointment.

She needed to focus on the reports she had in front of her, get ready for a meeting and prepare for a news conference on a recent toy recall. Later today she'd be standing in front of a group of reporters all waiting for her to slip up and give them something juicy to print, but she'd represent her company well. All she needed was a good night's sleep and to get her sexy neighbor out of her mind. Easier said than done.

2

RAFE HAD ACTUALLY MANAGED to doze on the sofa for a few hours come early morning. Waking to the sound of car doors slamming as people left for work, he'd made himself get up and had spent most of the day scraping the wallpaper from a small side room—nasty work in the heat—but it had kept him busy and active, and he'd accomplished something.

In spite of his lack of sleep and the hard work, he was charged with energy so he decided to go for a run. Endorphins, or the sun. Or a hint of his returning sex drive, maybe.

Though he'd shut the voice out last night, the simmering, sensual responses it sparked had lingered. He'd had to walk around the house several times to lose the morning erection that didn't seem to want to disappear. It was good to have blood pumping to those particular body parts again, though it would be nice if he had someone with whom to expend that excess energy.

The late-afternoon sun was setting low, and it still hit him as odd, but appealing, to be seeing summer sunsets in December. The news back home said the northeast was getting its first real snowstorm. Ambulances would be busy putting in extra hours; accidents, fires, all increased with the snow and ice. The kids would have a white Christmas, but for himself, he was content to have a sunny one. He heard the wail of sirens several times a day, and it never failed to make him look up for a second and wonder.

The beaches were a few miles from his neighborhood, and Warren had left a map in the car. San Diego was pretty easy to navigate, and he hopped in the car, taking the coastal highway a few miles north. He pulled off to the side and watched some late-day surfers decked out in neoprene paddle out into the water. He meant to look into taking some lessons—surfing seemed fun, and that was what he was here for: fun, recovery, relaxation. Hopefully a month of all three would get him back in shape to return to New York, and to his job. He got out of the car and started walking down the beach, falling into an easy jog.

He passed a group of young women in bikinis, their gazes following him as they watched him over the tops of their sunglasses. One smiled and offered a little wave. He nodded back and stopped jogging for a moment.

"Hey, why not?" He posed the question to himself under his breath and approached the beach bunnies, smiling at the girls as he neared.

"Hey, ladies."

"Hi there."

The one who'd waved had somehow claimed dibs, since the others backed off and let her take the lead. She was pretty—the kind of girl the Beach Boys sang about, what every New York man imagined California girls would be like. Blond, young, tanned all over.

"You talk like the guys on the *The Sopranos*."

"No, I don't." He laid on his New York accent a little heavier since they seemed to like it, though in truth it sounded more like the accents of the Italian kids he'd always hung out with, and still did. City accents weren't so much defined by where you were, but rather who you were, your ethnicity. As it turned out, Rafe was Italian-Irish, but he had more Italian speech patterns than Irish because of the neighborhood he'd grown up in.

Not that the beach bunny would care about the subtle distinctions of New York dialects. Or that Tony Soprano and his crime family actually lived in Essex County, in New Jersey.

They giggled again, and he was hopping from foot to foot, suddenly antsy instead of interested, ready to take off. The girls—and there was a world of difference between these girls and women his own age—were in their midtwenties, but seemed much younger. He was only thirty-three, but it seemed like a century from where they were. This had been a bad idea.

"You here on vacation?"

"Nope, just a regular working Joe, I'm afraid." He scowled—why did he lie?

Bunny pouted. "Too bad. You could blow off work and come party with us."

"Us?"

"All three of us, honey, if you're up for it." Her tone and the look she gave him left him in no doubt of what she meant. The prospect left him astoundingly cold. No doubt it would be the solution to his lack-of-sex problem—it could also potentially kill him—but he wasn't interested.

He had a certain sexy voice replaying in his mind like a TV jingle that wouldn't stop. His neighbor. Her voice seemed to get him going more than these girls.

"Sorry, gotta long day tomorrow, and have to get home. You ladies have a good evening."

He tipped an imaginary hat and walked away, thankful for an easy escape, and mentally kicking himself for stopping in the first place. Falling back into a run, he headed toward where he'd left Warren's car parked. He'd just been offered a deal most red-blooded, single men would have seriously considered. Instead of jumping at the opportunity, he was running in the other direction. Insomnia was neutering him.

Twenty minutes later he was driving through Balboa Park, taking a shortcut he'd found over to his neighborhood. Pulling into the driveway, he saw his neighbor, Ms. Talk-Dirty-To-Me, unloading something from her car. He was going to talk to her and deal with at least one of the things keeping him awake at night.

Taking the opportunity, he stopped by the curb near her driveway, got out and jogged up to where she was lifting bags out of the trunk. He checked her out—she had that natural look he liked on a woman, no makeup, pretty reddish-brown hair. A blue business suit disguised curves he could tell were hiding under its severe cut.

Her hair was clipped back tightly in a bun, though a few silky strands teased her neck, curling naughtily. His breath caught a little. What the hell? Was he having naughty-librarian fantasies about his neighbor? He cleared his throat, keeping his voice normal and friendly.

"Hi. Need a hand?"

He winced, hoping the simple question didn't sound like a pickup line.

Her gaze shot to him and then bolted away—she was working overtime not to make eye contact. Clearly she recognized him, but she was pretending not to. Why was she acting so weird?

"No, thanks."

"I'm your new neighbor—for a month, anyway."

"Yes, I know."

Wow, she was rude. Annoyed, considering it was *her* nighttime activities that were keeping him awake, he persisted, not willing to be pushed away so easily.

"Here, let me get that one—it looks heavy."

He reached to get the last paper sack, and she tried to beat him to the punch—the result being a large tear in the bag they both grabbed for, through which several canned items fell to the pavement, one narrowly missing his bare foot.

She was clearly agitated now. "I told you I didn't need you to do that—now look at what you did. These are all dented!"

He was going to apologize, hoping she found the accident more charming than angering, like something out of a romantic comedy. No such luck. She appeared truly distressed. Was she obsessive-compulsive in some way and couldn't tolerate dented cans?

"Does it taste different if the can is dented?" he joked, bending to help her pick them up, then stalled when her hand shot upward in a "stop" signal, halting him.

"These were to be donated to people at the local food bank. I don't want the families receiving them thinking someone would only donate damaged goods."

Her tone was scathing and Rafe stepped back. He had truly been trying to help. However, she had told him to back off, and he hadn't.

"I'm sorry. I'll tell you what, I'll take these and

replace them with new ones. Do you need them tonight?"

She was quiet for a moment, not meeting his eyes as she stood. "No, that's fine. Thank you. I can get some new ones in the morning."

"You and your boyfriend do a lot of charity work?" he asked, looking at her hand and not seeing a ring. "I can buy some groceries to contribute to the cause. To make up for being such a klutz." He tried the charming smile that he'd used at the beach. It didn't work on this woman. She glared.

"My boyfriend?"

She seemed confused, and that made him question his certainty.

"I assumed you were...involved." He decided to plunge forth with the conversation, taking the opportunity to address the issue he'd come to talk to her about. "I heard you two *talking*...you know, last night."

He put some slight emphasis on the words, trying to make obvious what he was really saying, but not wanting to embarrass her if he could help it. Though he'd like to see how she'd blush, what the effect would be on that pale skin. She shook her head, hitching her armful of bags up a little higher.

"I wasn't talking to anyone last night."

"Around two in the morning? It's why I hoped to catch you, actually. It was kind of loud, and I had a hard time sleeping. My bedroom window is right across from yours, so I, um, heard every word. I wasn't trying to eavesdrop, it was kind of unavoidable."

If she'd looked confused before, now she was staring at him as if he were certifiable.

"Listen, I don't know what you're going on about, but I wasn't talking to anyone, especially at that time of the night. I was dead asleep. The noise you heard must have been coming from somewhere else. Probably out on the street."

Now *he* was confused. Maybe she was embarrassed. That made sense, he figured—and hoped she was embarrassed enough to shut the window tonight.

"Hmm. Well, okay then. Are you sure I can't help you with those…?" He left the end of his sentence open, so she might fill in the blank with her name, the way most polite people would. Instead she frowned and turned up the walk.

"Yes. I'm sure."

Well, that had better solve his problem. Rafe went back to his house and hoped for the best.

THEY WERE WRAPPED in white satin, and everything was scented of rose petals and sex. Joy laughed—she was having the time of her life. *He* took a length of the smooth material and twisted it tight. Her heartbeat quivered in anticipation—what was he going to do?

"Hold out your arms," he commanded in a husky tone as smooth and hot as the undulating pleasure that was coursing through her bloodstream.

"Are you going to tie me up?"

"Yes. I want you helpless. *Mine.* To do whatever I want."

She quivered from head to toe, holding her hands up to him in supplication, but her thoughts were wicked.

"Do whatever you want to me—I want everything from you. Anything."

He laved her skin with his tongue as he wound the satin rope around her wrists in a soft figure eight, and then proceeded to bind her to her elbows. Gently, he pressed her back down, pushing her arms upward and attaching the ends of the material to the headboard.

"Anything?"

"Anything." She was daring, adventurous—she wanted to be the lover he'd never forget.

He rose up on his knees, glistening and perfect, his erection jutting out toward her belly as he swung one leg over, straddling her waist.

"You're so beautiful," he crooned, looking at her with eyes burning so fiercely she couldn't glance away. "You may be tied up, but I'm your slave. I'll do whatever gives you pleasure."

She writhed, arching upward, needing the contact he was promising, wanting the torture.

"I want to taste you. I want you in my mouth. You're so hard…. I love wrapping my lips around you when you're like this." The short, uneven pants of desire chopped her words into uneven phrases, but she didn't care.

"I think we can make that happen…. Your breasts are so full, so soft…."

He reached down, cupping her breasts. Leaning in, he sucked both nipples at once until she was nearly screaming with need as he licked her, wetting her skin all over, making her slick.

Straightening, he kept her breasts tight between his hands, torturing her nipples with his thumbs as he slid his cock in the pocket between, groaning, squeezing himself tighter as he thrust forward, toward her mouth.

She loved it, watching him start to lose control as he pumped faster. She dipped her chin to dart her tongue out, sliding it over the tip of him every time he moved forward, reveling in his guttural moan. He came fast and hard, and she drank in his excitement, helping him milk the last drop of ecstasy from his orgasm. She was so turned on she couldn't think straight.

He leaned in, kissing her forehead, and then moved down her body—she knew he wouldn't leave her unsatisfied. He never did.

Glancing up from between her parted thighs, one hand lightly pet the hair between her legs, the feathering touches almost making her beg. She fought her satiny restraints for the first time, wanting to gain control, to make him hurry.

Instead, he drew warm, wet trails up the inside of her thigh with his tongue, and then she did beg. Pleasure and need seeped from every pore as she strained toward him, her flesh parted for his invasion, exposing her.

His finger grazed her clit, drawing her body into one long shudder. He knew how to hold her back, laughing against her before his mouth descended. Her body bowed in taut anticipation of the release that was mere moments away, and she couldn't hold back a scream when she came, the name of her lover ripe on her lips. "Rafe."

RAFE WAS RIPPED AWAKE by the scream. He bolted out of bed, trying to discern the source—had he imagined it or had the woman's voice screamed his name?

The window—it had come from next door. Without much hesitation, he yanked on jeans, ran down the stairs and through the front door. Vaulting up his neighbor's steps, he banged on the door, yelling.

"Hey! You in there? You all right? Answer the door!"

He cursed that he'd left his cell back in the bedroom—if she didn't answer, he was calling 911.

He considered going down the side of the house and entering through the window, but he didn't know the situation. If things had gone bad—as they sometimes did between lovers, and who knew what his tidy and prim neighbor was into—he'd be walking blind into a crime scene. It could make a bad situation worse.

No one answered. He started back down the steps to go call the police when the door swung open, and he braced himself to face the guy who likely had caused the scream.

Instead he faced all five feet six inches or so of his neighbor, wrapped in a short terry robe that definitely showed off things the suit had been hiding earlier, including an absolutely gorgeous pair of legs. Her hair was wild, her face flushed. She looked as if she had been having sex; but she also looked furtive, and maybe a little frightened.

"What are you *doing?*" she demanded, taking a step back, closing the door slightly as if afraid of *him*—or blocking his sight of someone else standing there with her.

"I heard you scream—you called for help. You called my name."

It was dark on her porch though the light was on in the entry hall behind her. He squinted, taking a step closer, searching for bruises or any evidence of harm. Moving away, she started to close the door.

"I didn't scream, and I certainly didn't call for *you.*"

He didn't know why she would deny it, maybe she was embarrassed or maybe she was afraid. He knew from prior experience that someone could be behind her in the doorway, and she could be telling him to leave under some kind of duress. He had to see for himself that she was okay.

Clearly panicked, her voice rose. There was no way he was going anywhere until he knew what was up. "Leave me alone! I'm fine—are you crazy, coming to my door at this hour, causing trouble—"

"Okay, have it your way." He glanced at her, communicating his intention to get help, and went down the step.

"Wait."

He turned, watching her run a hand over her face. He wondered if she was covering for someone trying to escape from the back.

"Why should I let you in here when I'm alone—I don't even know you. For all I know this is some ploy to get inside the house."

He looked at her steadily. "Do intruders usually bang loudly on your door, shouting for everyone in the neighborhood to hear, and then talk to you on your front porch for a while?" He blew out a breath. "If I wanted in for some nefarious reason, believe me, this wouldn't be my method."

"I've seen stranger things on the news."

"I'm a friend of Warren's—doesn't that tell you something?"

"Not much. I don't know him that well."

"He lives right next door."

"So? Am I required to be best friends with my neighbors?"

Coming from a close-knit neighborhood, he shrugged—he'd always known his. Sometimes too well. Maybe things were different out here.

"Listen, I'm Warren's friend, and I'm also an EMT—though I don't have any ID at the moment—if you're hurt, I can help you, and you can call the police or I can, before I step foot in the place."

"Why do you keep insisting on thinking I'm hurt?"

"I told you, I heard you scream. It woke me up."

"I'm telling you, it wasn't me." She bit the words out, increasingly agitated, but he knew what he'd heard.

Had she really screamed his name? Out loud? The thought had her cringing inwardly.

"It *was* you. What I want to know is why you're lying. It's either me or the police, sweetheart, take your pick."

Furious, she threw open the door, challenging him, and he had a moment of doubt. Still, he needed to follow through—he had to make sure she was okay, then he'd leave.

JOY WATCHED HER NEIGHBOR—she still didn't even know his name—as he prowled around her home. He'd given her one of the most intimate visual inspections she'd ever experienced before he'd started checking out the house. He said he was an EMT, and she supposed his survey was strictly clinical, though it hadn't felt that way. Given what she'd been dreaming about, that could be her fault, but she wouldn't admit it.

He hadn't laid a hand on her; he'd done nothing inappropriate, but had looked her over so thoroughly, apparently searching for signs of abuse, that she'd nearly squirmed. He was in her bedroom now, convincing himself she was safe. Her cheeks went up in flames.

She was mortified and impressed all at once that he was so concerned about her safety. Not all neighbors were willing to get involved. She never was. It wasn't anything personal, but she worked a lot, and had never really gotten to know the people living around her. Still, had she really been in trouble, she was glad to know there was someone who would help.

However, this situation was getting more embarrassing by the minute. She must have screamed in her sleep the way she had in the dream—in her dream about *him*—but there was no way she was admitting that. She supposed she could have claimed to have had a nightmare, but that wouldn't explain screaming his name. She wasn't exactly good at thinking on her feet in the middle of the night. She hoped that once he saw there was no one else in the house, he'd believe her that he'd heard a voice from some other source.

As he ran up the stairs, two at a time, she couldn't stop the rush of heat that flowed right down her spine to her core as she watched the muscles in his back flex, and she almost sighed over the perfect masculine shape of his rear. This man was even more handsome up close than he was in her dreams.

And, in her dreams, he had been perfect.

She shook her head, trying to clear her mind.

When he came back down, he gazed at her with curiosity and announced, "You seem to be here alone."

"Yes, I told you that."

"So why'd you scream?"

"No, I… It wasn't me. It must have been someone out on the street."

He shook his head, and then his eyes narrowed. She held her breath—what was he thinking?

"Do you talk in your sleep?"

It was as if her deepest secret had been revealed—which in a way it had—and she shook her head in denial.

"No. No one's ever said so, anyway."

"That has to be it. You must have been having a dream or something—do you remember?"

She crossed her arms defensively. "No, I don't. I was sleeping soundly until you came slamming at the door, demanding access to my home, threatening me with the police."

There. The best defense was a good offense, right?

"I thought you were in trouble. It was a pretty loud scream. Woke me out of a…a halfway decent sleep." His tone took on a tenor of astonishment. "I can't believe I was actually *sleeping,* and then you woke me up," he accused.

Her "good offense" strategy was suddenly on the ropes. "Listen, I don't know what it was, but I'd like to get back to sleep, and I assume you would, too."

They were standing about a foot apart, and all she had on was her robe and underwear. From what she could tell, all he had on were those jeans, and they weren't even zipped up all the way. She had to get him out of here before she almost swooned for crying out loud, feeling a surge of lust for him.

"I won't be able to get back to sleep."

"Why not?"

"I have chronic insomnia, and the nightly chatter hasn't been helping. I can't remember the last time I actually was sleeping as soundly as I was before your scream ended that."

"I. Didn't. Scream," she ground out between her teeth. "I don't talk all night. I don't talk in my sleep."

He ran a hand though sandy hair that was cut just the right length, and the gesture made her lose her train of thought for a moment. He had perfect arms. Nicely toned, muscular but not ridiculously so. They were manly arms. She didn't like the body-builder type, though she had no doubt he was strong. What on earth was she doing? She never— or rarely—ogled men like this.

"Listen, fine. You probably don't snore either, but—"

"Hey! I *don't* snore," she declared stoutly. This much she knew for sure.

"Fine. Still, on the very small, almost impossible chance that it's you, and that you don't realize it, could you do me a favor and close your window? Just in case."

The sarcasm of his tone put her off, but even if it hadn't, she wasn't about to change her habits for a stranger.

"No."

He blinked, standing there looking luscious and confused. Images of what he'd done to her earlier in her dream ran through her head like an X-rated movie, and she had to drop her gaze.

"*No?* Just like that?"

"It's hot."

"Use your AC."

"I don't have AC. There's only one small window unit in the house and it is too noisy. Why don't you close your window?"

"Why should I close my windows? You're the one screaming in the middle of the night."

She squared her jaw, supposing there was no reason not to tell the truth on this one. "Well, I'm not closing my window either—it's too hot."

"Fine."

"Fine."

She stifled a yawn, moving toward the door. "I don't know who you've been hearing at night, but people are out on the streets all the time—it was probably something out there."

"It's the same voice, saying the same things. In fact, it's your voice. I'm sure of it."

Sending him what she thought was the coldest look she could manage, she yanked open the door. "You're imagining things. Thanks for your concern, but I'd like to go back to bed."

He moved toward the door, shaking his head, and looking at her with a smile that had her knees buckling. Then she caught herself.

"I'm Rafe by the way. Rafe Moore," he said slowly, watching her closely as if to catch her up, and she hoped she gave nothing away.

"Good night, Mr. Moore."

She didn't offer her own name, and simply arched an eyebrow when he paused, waiting. Blowing out a breath, he nodded once, his lips tightening. She almost felt bad, but she didn't want to give him one ounce of encouragement.

"Call me Rafe. We're neighbors, after all. Good night."

Joy sank down by the door, utterly mortified. She'd held her own, but her dreams were obviously getting out of control.

Rafe wasn't the only one who wouldn't be going back to sleep tonight. In truth, she hated that she was contributing to his insomnia. He seemed nice, really, and was obviously a good guy, concerned about his neighbors, ready to help. He had a really cute accent, too….

Shaking away thoughts of her hunky neighbor, Joy couldn't risk going back to bed and the dreams starting up again. Not tonight. She didn't know why she was having them—she didn't even care for sex all that much. The few serious relationships she'd had had proved that. Of course, maybe if sex in reality was as terrific as it was in her unconscious, she'd revise her opinion, but in her experience, it hadn't been.

Eyeing the armchair and ottoman by the TV from her sitting position at the base of the door, she smiled. At least if she fell back into her lusty dreams no one would hear her from there.

3

RAFE SEARCHED THE CROWDED shelves of the garage in the corner where Warren kept his tools. He was looking for the laser level Warren had bragged about, but couldn't find it anywhere. His pal was not a slob, exactly, but he was a pack rat. Everything from old electrical tape to plastic bags with every spare part you could think of was crammed three-deep on the narrow shelves.

While Rafe hadn't been able to fall back asleep, the couple hours he'd managed had given him a boost of energy. He was intent on repainting the small kitchen for Warren and his bride—Rafe's version of a Christmas/wedding gift—but he had to put up the wainscoting first, and that required the level.

When he yanked free a box from an upper shelf, what he found was more interesting—an older model camcorder. He recognized it in an instant—Warren had gotten it for his eighteenth birthday, and they'd had a hell of a time with it.

They'd pestered Rafe's sisters particularly, following them around with the camera until his eldest sister, Becky, had threatened to crush it under her car wheel if they didn't stop. Rafe was the fourth after three sisters, and though he loved them dearly, and they all had close relationships now, back then, he had been a major pain, as younger brothers aim to be.

Taking the camcorder out, Rafe saw there was a tape inside and for the heck of it, hit the play button, wondering if he might stumble across one of those old adventures. Within seconds, he was hitting the off button, a little shocked—Warren and his new wife had apparently been having a little fun with home movies back before they were married and had forgotten to remove the tape. Of course, they probably hadn't expected anyone to be rummaging through their garage, either.

His embarrassment at discovering the video of Warren in flagrante delicto was muted by the sudden brainstorm that hit him—this could be just what he needed to prove his case.

If his neighbor, name still unknown, wouldn't believe she was talking—and loudly—in her sleep, he could tape her and prove it. Then, she wouldn't be able to deny it was her.

He took the tape out. He could buy a new one and replace this one later, after he accomplished his purpose. There was a place downtown that converted old tapes to compact discs. If he went to the local hardware store now, he could buy a new tape and a level to work on the kitchen.

However, grabbing Warren's keys and heading out to the car—which always stayed in the driveway because the garage was far too packed with everything for it to fit—Rafe was distracted by an older woman teetering on a ladder across the street, hanging some Christmas lights. He jogged over, looking up and calling out, "Hello. That ladder seems a little rickety—could I give you a hand with those lights?"

The woman suspiciously looked down at him. "Who are you?"

He smiled. She reminded him a lot of his grandmother, whom he especially missed at Christmas. This woman seemed tough and independent as well; Rafe recognized the look.

"Rafe Moore, ma'am, at your service. I'm watching over Warren and Trudy's house while they're on their honeymoon."

"Oh, I have seen you. Warren, he's a good boy."

Watching her twist around on the ladder Rafe got nervous.

"If you would like, I could give you a hand with those lights. That ladder doesn't seem too stable. Warren has a good one in the garage. Why don't you come down and let me go get it?"

She smiled. "That would be wonderful."

Rafe moved forward, holding the ladder firmly as she started to step down, relieved he'd come outside when he had—if she'd fallen, it could have been serious, even from only six feet up. On the job, he'd frequently been called for older people who'd taken simple falls in their own houses, falls that had caused their deaths in some cases.

"What's your name, ma'am?"

"Oh, sorry, I'm Bessie Woods." She lowered herself slowly. Finally with both feet on the ground, she smiled up at Rafe, shaking her head at the ladder. "My husband passed on last spring. I didn't really plan to do much for the holiday. My family is worried and doesn't want me alone, so I just found out they're all coming here next week to spend a few days before Christmas. I'll go home with them for the New Year. I couldn't have the grandkids showing up with not a single Christmas light on the house."

She sounded a little grumpy. Rafe nodded, straightening the ladder, silently cheering her family for not abandoning their matriarch. She might not think she wanted the Christmas cheer and the company, but she'd be happier for it once everyone was around. The holidays were so hard for people who'd lost loved ones.

"Well, let's see what we can do about that."

She patted his arm and moved to the side so he could remove the ladder from where it leaned against the porch.

"We'll do that, and then you can come in and I'll make you some lunch." She didn't ask him, she told him, and he chuckled, not even bothering to argue. She looked up at the ladder.

"My Butch had that ladder for years. I was always yelling at him to get a new one or he'd break his neck. He never did, so I figured it must be good enough. Have to admit, though, I miss him every day. He used to take care of all these things, and…" Her voice faded, choking slightly, and Rafe's heart squeezed.

"How long were you married?"

"Fifty-seven years. Four children of our own, eleven grandkids, four great grands," she declared proudly, and Rafe was doing some quick math in his head.

"They're all coming for Christmas?" He looked at the small house, wondering how they'd fit.

She laughed. "Oh, no, just my youngest son's family—he lives the closest. The rest are scattered all over the country, though I see them often enough."

"Good to have a close family," he stated and realized for the first time that he actually was spending the first Christmas without his own. For some reason, his urge to escape the city, and the job, had blanked out that realization. He knew they'd understand—he'd missed several holidays when he'd had to work—but he'd never been away, completely, for the entire time. His sisters were busy, too—two of them were married; the other, a single lawyer, didn't seem to have much interest in marriage.

The four of them were always in and out of their parents' house, around the neighborhood, several times each week. None of them had ever considered leaving New York. It had been a shock for them when Rafe had announced he was heading to California, if only for a little more than a month. They'd been apprehensive, but supportive. They knew he was having problems, and he knew they were only a phone call away.

His eyes drifted over across the street, to his neighbor's house. Did she have family? People who cared? She appeared to be very alone. He felt a twinge of sympathy if that was the case.

"Where are you from, Rafe?" Bessie interrupted his thought.

"New York City."

"Ah, been there once. Too loud for me."

He laughed. "Bessie, what do you think about giving this ladder to the Goodwill—they'll repair it for someone else's use, and we can get you a sturdier stepping stool, though not for outside jobs.

"That sounds like a smart idea."

He looked over at the house next to Warren's where nothing was stirring.

"Can I ask you a question, Bessie?"

"Depends on what it is."

"Do you know the name of the woman across the street?"

She eyed him shrewdly. "That's Joy Clarke."

Joy, he thought, liking the name. He'd never known a Joy before.

"As far as I know, she's free as a bird," Bessie added knowingly. "Used to be a young man who visited pretty often, stayed some nights, if his car in the driveway is any indication, but that was a while ago. I didn't like him."

"You met?"

"No, but I didn't like how he came speeding up the street in his fancy car, the radio blasting. A real man doesn't need to draw attention to himself like that. She doesn't have much to do with anyone, from what I can tell. Probably has her reasons. She does come around collecting for charity now and then, but that's about it. I don't know much, but I do know you look like a man who's interested."

He pulled back. "No, no...not *that* way. There's a neighbor issue I need to talk to her about. Thought it would go easier if I knew her name, at least."

"Whatever you say."

It was clear Bessie wasn't buying his story, though he took her teasing in good humor. She hustled in to make the promised lunch—and to get more lights now that she had someone to help hang them. He went to get Warren's ladder, and wondered about Joy as he strung the lights. He noticed there wasn't a single holiday decoration in her yard.

Bessie served him one of the best bowls of chicken soup he'd ever had, even if it did make him sweat in the sweltering heat. Cooling off, relatively speaking, he sat on the step out front untangling some outdoor extension cords he'd found in Warren's garage. Joy emerged, looking as if she were going somewhere, keys in hand, and he decided to make another approach.

"Joy!" he called from across the street, setting the cords down and seeing she was surprised he knew her name. Crossing to meet her, he tried to ignore the way she tensed up when he neared.

"Sleeping in late on Saturday, huh?"

"I've been busy. How'd you know my name?"

"Bessie mentioned it."

"Bessie?"

He tilted his head toward the house across the street. "Bessie? The older lady who lives there, in the white house—just lost her husband?"

"Oh, yes. Right."

"I caught her trying to hang some Christmas lights and almost killing herself up on a ladder, so I'm helping her out. Wondered if you might want to come over and give us a hand? I could use someone on the ground to feed me the extension cord while I'm up on the roof. She makes a mean chicken soup."

"Sorry, I have to get going. I need to replace those groceries." She didn't bother hiding the stiff accusation in her tone. "And run some errands."

"Don't you ever relax?"

She was clearly taken aback. "I beg your pardon?"

"You're always so tense, so tight. You'll give yourself high blood pressure."

She arched an eyebrow. "I guess you're an expert, seeing as you're an EMT?"

He smiled. "You remembered."

"Impossible to forget conversations with men who storm in my door in the middle of the night."

"I hardly stormed your door. Though I probably would have if you hadn't answered."

"That's not comforting."

"I thought you were in trouble. I didn't know you were talking in your sleep," he added, his normally easygoing personality giving way to the urge to taunt her.

"I do not—never mind. I have to get going."

She stepped around him, and he let her go, shaking his head, but thanking her silently for the reminder that he still needed to go to the store to pick up that tape.

"I DON'T KNOW WHAT I'D DO without you, Joy— you're a total lifesaver."

"I had fun. The guys did most of the heavy lifting, and I can't wait to get back and get those chairs and dressers cleaned up—they're really gorgeous. You might want to consider selling them rather than using them—I think at least one is an antique."

They'd been moving some furniture donated by

an estate sale into the Second Chance shelter that Pam ran, and were taking time out for a late lunch. It had been a busy afternoon.

"Oh, I don't know. I kind of like the idea of replacing some of the crappier stuff, make the rooms nicer."

Joy grinned, relaxed for the first time in days as she sat with Pam Reynolds at the cheery sidewalk café, munching panini sandwiches and talking. Pam was the first friend she'd made in San Diego after she'd moved. The people who had owned Joy's house had left some old furniture, and Joy had been looking for a place to donate the stuff. She'd discovered a shelter a half mile away and when she'd called Pam, she'd not only taken Joy's donations, but had ended up talking her into doing some volunteer time at the shelter.

It was a great place. Second Chance did more than give people a meal or a cot for the night; Pam was really trying to change people's lives. The shelter housed up to twelve residents at a time. The men came from all walks of life, but they all wanted a second chance, and that was what she gave them. Pam had arrangements with local colleges, employers, businesses, high schools, doctors…. Whatever it took to give a break to those who were willing to work for it.

Joy had been so inspired by the project that she'd become a regular volunteer and supporter. Even when she was involved in the most menial tasks, Joy was doing something real, something worthwhile. She was contributing to people's lives. She spent a lot of her weekend and weeknight time at the shelter, helping out how she could, but also visiting with Pam. They'd become close friends over the years. Though Pam was about ten years older than Joy, the age difference meant nothing to their friendship.

A San Diego native, Pam hardly looked her age either; her curly hair, almost black, framed skin kissed by the California sun. Pam's family lived in an exclusive neighborhood northeast of the city, and she'd been born into privilege that no one would imagine given her no-nonsense clothes, almost always jeans and T-shirts. She was pretty, but didn't bother with makeup; she almost didn't need to. Joy envied her strong features and flawless skin.

"Any chance you can cover me tonight for a few hours?" Pam asked tentatively and then waved her hand. "Never mind. You've been working all day, and it's Saturday night."

"You have a hot date?" Joy teased.

Then the most amazing thing happened: Pam's beautiful skin turned beet-red. Joy's jaw dropped.

"You do! You're seeing him again, aren't you, this mystery man you've been stealing away with…."

"Oh stop that—we're not 'stealing away' anywhere. It's simply a Saturday night out."

"With the same guy?"

Pam seemed very tense, and Joy didn't get it.

They usually talked about everything, including men, but on the topic of her love life, Pam was unusually silent. Joy didn't push, but it was the single snag in their friendship that she worried about; why wouldn't Pam confide in her? Wasn't that what best friends did? Joy told Pam everything, not that there was much to tell—she'd dated some guys from work, but nothing much ever came of it.

"Sorry, I didn't mean to push. I just want you to know you can talk to me if you need to."

Pam smiled. "I know that. I will tell you about him, once I know how it's all going to work out."

"It's been going on for a while—you guys getting serious? Wait—sorry—I didn't ask that," Joy said, holding her hand up, and they laughed. "If you want a night off, I can cover for you. I don't have any plans tonight," Joy offered.

"I wish you did." Pam made the comment offhandedly as she polished off the last of her salad.

"What's that supposed to mean?"

Pam sighed, pushing her plate back. "Joy, you're a jewel and I'm so thankful we met I can't tell you. It just seems like you don't do anything but work and volunteer at the shelter. It's not healthy."

"I do plenty of other things."

"Like what? I think you've only been out on a dozen dates in the entire six years I've known you."

"I date now and then, but I can't seem to meet anyone who catches my interest. They're all so…I don't know, they're just not guys I want to go out with more than once or twice."

"Maybe because you worked with most of them and you ended up talking shop most of the time. You should be fishing in different oceans. Find someone new, with a different job, different interests?"

"Maybe. I don't know, Pam. I've tried the whole dating thing, but I don't seem to have the same wiring as other women."

"Meaning?"

"You know. I've told you." Joy lowered her voice and leaned across the table. "I'm no good at any of it. Dating, men, sex…I never have been."

"You're being too tough on yourself. You just haven't met the right guy."

Joy pushed her own sandwich away, unfinished, and met Pam's eyes. "You don't want to talk about your love life, I don't see why mine has to be under the microscope."

"Now stop being like that. I'm your friend. I want what's best for you. I told you, I'll tell you everything soon, but for now, I want to hear if you've met anyone new."

"Not really, I mean… Well," she hedged, thinking of her sexy neighbor.

"C'mon, I know there's some dirt you're not telling me. Fess up."

Joy sighed and relented. "I, apparently, talk in

my sleep. Loudly and clearly," she added with sarcastic gusto.

"What does that have to do with—wait—is this something a man told you? Someone who might have spent the night, perhaps?"

"Yes, no—I mean, not exactly."

"You only had a soda with lunch, right?" Pam teased, and Joy stuck out her tongue at her.

"It's complicated."

"It always is. Do you always talk in your sleep?"

"I'm not sure, but…"

Fighting a strangling sense of mortification, Joy went on to tell Pam about the dreams—and her sexy neighbor's visit in the middle of the night. She hoped for some sympathy, but by the time she was done relating the tale, Pam was smiling broadly, and…laughing.

"This isn't funny." Joy wrapped her arms around her middle and became mulish, not enjoying her friend's amusement at her expense.

"I'm sorry, honey, but it kinda is. I mean, you've been losing sleep dreaming sexy dreams about this guy, and he's hearing it through his window. He's getting a blow-by-blow, er, you know what I mean. Now he shows up at your door, your knight in shining armor? Ready to take on the guy who made you scream—and that happens to have been *him,* at least in your dream? No, this is *very* funny. It's exactly what you need."

"You're losing your mind. No one needs this. I'm exhausted, I forgot a meeting the other day, and Ken was completely pissed. I'm up for that promotion, and that didn't help. I do not need another guy in my life right now."

"Maybe not in your life, but you could definitely use one in your bed. There is a difference. Is this new guy hot?"

Joy made a face. "Very. He seems like a nice enough guy, too—he did come over to 'rescue' me when he thought I was in trouble. He was helping the older lady across the street with her Christmas decorations. I think I heard him working on Warren's, my neighbor's, house."

"A real live Boy Scout."

"Would make sense. He's an EMT. Used to saving people."

"Sounds like he's always prepared," Pam added naughtily, and Joy couldn't resist laughing, her bad mood melting away as she joined in the joke.

"He did do a good job with tying knots in my dream."

The two women dissolved in laughter.

"I think you should go for it."

"Go for what?"

"He heard you talking—and we can only imagine what you're saying—and he's coming around, trying to strike up conversations, hoping to save you from dastardly deeds…checking to see if you're attached. He's *interested,* Joy. So be interested back. Have a fling. Give yourself a hottie for Christmas."

Heat invaded Joy's face. "No way. Just because I'm having these dreams, that doesn't translate into reality."

Pam shoved her chair back and stood, leaving a tip on the table. "Maybe it should. He sounds like a perfect man—hot, willing and temporary. If you're doing him instead of dreaming about him, maybe you'll actually get some sleep. In fact, scratch tonight—I want you to get some rest."

"Please, keep your date. I'm fine, and I love being a part of what you do," Joy said with sincere emotion in her voice, trying to avoid the temptation to think too much about Pam's idea.

"I do, too, in spite of the problems lately. We lost a major source of funding last week. All the businesses are strapping down the coffers with the economy in the shape it is. They have less to give, even at this time of year, and you know this is when we count on receiving our big donations."

"Is it serious? I can't imagine this place closing—it's too valuable to the community."

"No, we won't close, but we might lose some essential resources if I can't pull something together."

"I guess asking your folks…?"

Pam shook her head resolutely. "No. They never approved of me doing this. While we manage to have a halfway decent relationship, there's no way I would ask them for money, and they wouldn't give it anyway."

Joy's heart went out to her friend. "I'll do whatever I can to help, Pam."

"You're a sweetheart, Joy. I wish I could afford to put you on as paying staff at Second Chance for all the work you do, but it's not possible at this point."

"I don't need the money—that's why I have a job. I'll pound the pavement, do whatever I can to help you get this place in the black."

Joy teared up. She didn't know why this was affecting her so strongly.

"Thanks, I'll take you up on that. I hope you'll also think about doing whatever you need for yourself, as well. Give yourself a gift."

Joy rolled her eyes, realizing Pam was back on their previous topic.

"I promise I'll think about it," she said, knowing that she likely wasn't going to be thinking about anything else.

4

EARLY MONDAY MORNING, Rafe slipped the disk he'd had converted from the camcorder tape into a paper bag and rolled down the top of the bag with determination. He'd leave it for her with a note. She'd find and listen to it. Then there would be no denying that she was not only sleep-talking, but she was dreaming about him.

Why she would be, he had no idea. Joy was pretty, and he'd admit she wasn't hard to look at, but she hardly seemed interested—in fact, she seemed the direct opposite of interested. Yet, she had screamed his name in her sleep. He was sure of it. He'd tried to replay it a thousand times, wondering if he misheard or imagined it, but the next night had told the truth—she'd done it again, and he'd gotten the evidence.

He eyed the bag, thoughts simmering in his brain. His major goal was to win—to prove to her that he was right, and that he wasn't just harassing her. Her attitude toward him all but made him sound like a liar or a perve, and he didn't like either one.

Still, there were other possibilities. What if she dropped the argument, and apologized? What if she admitted the truth? What if she really was attracted to him—that would explain the nighttime fantasies, right? Question was, was he interested back? Maybe. It had been a long time since he'd had sex, or had even been in the mood. When Joy Clarke was in dream mode, her sexy talk got him going, and he might be willing to explore that, if the circumstances were right.

A zing of interest worked through him, unexpected, but welcome. This kind of thing was exactly what vacations were for.

He finished the note and smiled. All set. He didn't have any plans for today, so he'd hang out here, work on the house and see what happened. Peering out the window, he saw her car in the front drive—she hadn't left for work yet. Good.

Quickly darting out the door and across the short yard, he left the package on her step, inside the screen door so she wouldn't miss it.

He thought he heard her singing some top-forty song through the open screen, her voice becoming slightly louder, definitely off-key. Cute.

She was walking toward the front door. After running back to his own porch, he ducked behind a tall plant, watching her come outside, notice the package. She picked it up and looked around, pausing for a moment; he swore she was looking right at him, but she couldn't possibly see him through the thick foliage.

She opened the envelope, read the note with a roll of her eyes and shoved the disk into her bag. *Score!*

Smugly satisfied that she would be stopping by later to apologize and imagining how graciously he'd accept, Rafe thought he might invite her out to get a bite to eat. From there, the possibilities were endless.

IT HAD BEEN A COMPLETELY crappy morning.

Joy slid her fingers through her hair as she worked on news spots for the recall follow-ups and knew her mind wasn't on it. She kept making stupid spelling errors as she composed an e-mail form response to all the angry customers writing the company. She looked at what she'd written in a fit of pique:

Dear Valued Carr Toys Customer:
We at Carr Toys value your business and continued patronage. As complaints go, the wheels falling off a toy is not an earth-shattering problem, so please get over it and stop bothering me. I haven't had a decent night's sleep in weeks, and I'm really getting tired of your constant complaints about such a trivial issue. Have a nice day, and we hope you'll continue to shop Carr Toys.

Yeah, that would probably need to be heavily revised.

"Problem?"

Ken, the PR director, peeked in her office door, and pasting on a smile, she shook her head.

"No, no problem. I've been working on the latest e-mail response to the Toddler Tank complaints."

"Didn't I tell you? Barb's handling that since she was in that meeting you missed."

The slight note of censure was there, and Joy hated herself for being unnerved by it.

"I'm sorry, Ken. It won't happen again."

He stepped inside her door, looking down at the folders in his hand, then back at her.

"Joy, you've been acting strangely lately. You should take a break. You've got a lot of vacation time piled up."

"Ken, I'll get back on my game. I have no desire for time off. I wouldn't know what to do with myself." She laughed lightly, hoping he was buying it. "I live for my work."

Her boss eyed her speculatively, as if he were about to say something, and then nodded.

"Okay, if you say so. I'd rather have you take some time off than not be able to give one hundred percent."

As if she didn't usually give one hundred and twenty? Wasn't she due an eighty-percent day now and then? She nearly had to bite her tongue to stop from reminding him that she'd missed one meeting—one, in the entire time she'd worked there. Exhausted, she'd overslept and hadn't made it in until noon. Yes, that was bad, but it wasn't as if she made a habit of it.

"Gotcha. No problem." She forced a smile.

When he was gone, she sagged in her chair. It was lunchtime, but she had too much to do, and she wanted to catch up and get back in the swing. It had to be the loss of sleep; she'd never been so dragged out.

Maybe saying she lived for work was an overstatement, but she certainly wasn't as on top of things as she should be, and she wanted that promotion—more money, a bigger office, more job security, and her father would be very proud of her. Maybe once that was accomplished, she could take a vacation. After she'd established herself in the new position, of course.

Her stomach growled. She should see if there were any bagels left in the snack room down the hall. Grabbing her purse, she walked to the outer offices. Reaching inside it to find some change, her hands touched something unfamiliar. Then she remembered shoving the disk in there earlier.

Sitting down at a computer kiosk, she heard muted voices behind her and turned. The representatives of some new potential distributors were congregating outside Ken's office, getting ready to leave for lunch.

She glanced at the masculine scrawl on the plain white paper, frowning. It was obviously from her neighbor—what was he up to? The note simply read: *Play this when you get a chance. Thanks, Rafe. PS: I'm flattered.*

It was mysterious and annoying, and she flipped the shiny disk out of its package and slid it into the computer in front of her. What could her neighbor be up to now? Why couldn't he just leave her alone? Still, curiosity got the better of her. He said he was flattered—flattered about what?

Squinting, it appeared to be a video, though not a very clear one. There was no image, only a dark smudge that looked like some kind of night shot, and the picture wasn't good at all, but the sound was exceedingly clear.

"Oh, God, yes…there…harder…"

The sultry voice filled the room, and Joy sat back in total shock—it sounded like *her.*

"You're so hard…. Rafe, I need you inside me…."

Realizing it *was* her, she sprang furiously into action, hitting the keyboard frantically and trying to shut the damned thing off, but somehow, due to the magic of computer technology and recalcitrant fingers, she ended up turning the volume up even louder instead. The room was ringing with moans and sighs. The sound triggered a memory, and she knew exactly what was coming next.

"Oh, no! Stop! I said stop!" She yelled at the console, hitting the button on the little disk slot repeatedly, trying to extricate the disk before it was too late.

Finally the slot popped open, and she removed the disk with shaking fingers, thankfully cutting short some of the more graphic descriptions of how much she loved Rafe's…equipment.

My God, she thought, totally mortified. She'd never even thought half of the words she'd heard coming out of her mouth, let alone *said* them.

Disk in hand, she didn't look up for a few minutes, afraid of what she might find. When she did, her first reaction was gratitude that most of the people had left for lunch. However, the few lingering workers—including one freshman college intern—were all staring at her.

Words of profuse apology forming on her lips, she recalled the distributors and closed her eyes in mortal agony. The sound of someone clapping loudly startled everyone back to life. A sick sense of dread punched her in the gut. She turned to find the men all staring at her, too, some smiling widely. Ken looked horrified.

Unable to process what had just happened, Joy fumbled the disk back into her purse and headed for her office. Slamming the door behind her, she leaned against her desk, trying to catch her breath, but finding it difficult. Ken came in behind her.

"What the hell was that?" Then he backed off, looking at her more closely. "Joy—what happened? Are you going to faint?"

Joy wasn't sure, actually—she'd never fainted in

her life, but she was tempted to give it a shot. The black world of unconsciousness was pretty appealing right now.

"I d-don't know," she panted, trying to get hold of her panicked breathing.

"How can you not know?"

"I don't know," she bit out. "Someone left me that disk and I didn't know what was on it." She could at least tell the truth about that much. Her PR instincts kicked in. She had to find a way to make this better.

"You should call security."

"No, no. I think I know who it was. I'll handle it. It was a joke, I'm sure."

"A pretty sick joke. I'll support you in placing a formal complaint against whoever gave it to you."

"No. I mean, it wasn't anyone here—it was at home. I found it in my mailbox."

Ken stood gaping, unsure what to say. Obviously he hadn't equated the voice on the recording with her, which was no surprise. When people thought of her, they didn't exactly think "sex kitten," and her normal voice was nothing like the sultry, sexy voice on the recording. Even she had trouble believing it was her, but it was. No need for Ken to know that, though.

"Ken, please, I'm okay. You have people waiting," she reminded him. She just had to get him out of there.

"Shit, yeah. I'll tell them it was a bad joke, and we're handling it."

"That's good. That's about right. Extend my deepest apologies."

"I'll do that." He looked at her for one moment longer, and she started messing with the folders on her desk, waiting until he walked back out the door.

Crisis averted, hopefully. Still, it was akin to when the jury heard evidence that they weren't supposed to—someone could tell them to erase it, but she knew this would become part of office lore, and remain on Ken's mind for a while. She was going to have to kick butt on her presentation to get that promotion.

Armed with that resolve, Joy tried to get back to work. Her concentration lasted about five minutes.

How could he have done this? Her neighbor seemed like such a nice guy, but apparently he was a big pervert who taped women in their sleep.

Well, okay, maybe not a pervert, she admitted grudgingly. She supposed she had pushed him into proving his point, since she wouldn't cowboy up about the sleep-talking. Yet what he'd done was wrong, and intrusive, and it had given her some bad moments at work. She was going to get through this afternoon and then she planned on making her neighbor her first order of business when she got home.

RAFE WAS HAVING a great day—one of the best he'd had in a long while. After a relaxing morning run, he'd finished up a few projects. He wondered what

Joy was thinking as she listened to his video. Sure she'd grouse about being proved wrong in her denials of sleep-talking, but he hoped she'd be good-natured about it.

In the late afternoon he decided to wash Warren's car. Several kids were playing football in the street. When the ball was tossed into his driveway, he pretended not to notice, but then turned the hose on the kid who bravely came after the ball. A frenzied water fight ensued. The kids abandoned their game in search of supersoaking water pistols, camping out behind the bushes, making sneak attacks as they plotted to get the best of him.

Though he adored his sisters, Rafe always loved the horseplay with his male buddies that he didn't get at home. The kids' eyes shone with delight when he blasted them with the hose. Kids loved water, and they loved play-combat, and that was the same no matter what coast you were on.

When he heard a sound behind him, he growled playfully and swung around. Gripping the trigger on the nozzle, he hosed the figure standing on the other side of the driveway—but it wasn't one of the kids, and he released the hose trigger immediately, the jet stream of water flagging to a drizzle. Too late.

"Oh, shit...Joy, I'm so sorry...." He heard the chuckles and catcalls of young boys behind him as they delighted in his mistake. "I thought you were one of the kids…. You know, we don't always think in the heat of battle."

She stared at him silently, her lips pressed tightly together, her eyes cool—no, make that frosty. She was soaked from the blast; water was dripping down her cheeks.

"Are you okay? I, uh, didn't see you there."

She choked out a little laugh, one that didn't sound humorous—this woman looked as if she was teetering on the edge. What he knew from growing up in a house with three sisters was that her black cloud of temper was centered on him, and it was about far more than getting soaked with a hose. His mind zipped to the tape and he intuited that it might not have gone over as well as he'd hoped.

A few silly comments were still floating around the yard, and he waved his hand behind him, shooing the kids away. They complied, groaning about their fun ending, but Rafe was focused only on Joy and how she was continuing to glare at him.

"How could you?" she finally said, her voice tight and low.

"I told you, I didn't know it was you…."

"You *know* that's not what I mean. This—" she looked down at her sopping-wet suit before continuing "—is adding insult to injury. What were you hoping to accomplish? Embarrass me? Get me fired? Is this some kind of sick revenge for your sleep problems?"

He frowned, dropping the hose and stepping forward. "Revenge? For what? What are you talking about—why did you get fired?"

"I didn't get fired, but no thanks to you and your stupid...that awful...that..."

She couldn't seem to say the words. Much to his dismay, she choked back a sound that was half sob, half moan, which only seemed to add to her embarrassment as she lifted her hands to her face, her shoulders starting to quake.

"Oh, no! Joy—you played that at *work?*"

He thought back, remembering how she'd popped the disk in her bag. Never in his wildest imagination had he thought she'd play it anywhere public. He looked up—she made next to no sound, holding it all in, but her stiff shoulders hunched and he knew she was deeply upset. It struck him that what he'd done had been thoughtless, and he'd been so smug about it all day. He was ashamed about that; what had seemed like a good idea now appeared so stupid. Taking a step forward, he started to speak, and when she lowered her hands, her eyes were blazing.

"Yes, I took it to work, you son of a bitch! I didn't know what it was. I didn't know some lowdown Peeping Tom had videotaped me sleeping—what are you, some kind of sicko?"

Low-down? Peeping Tom?

"Now hold on just one second—I never intended for you to go and—"

"Oh, so now this is *my* fault?" She wiped the tears from her eyes furiously, and he didn't know what to say. This wasn't exactly the end he'd imagined.

"No, but I didn't know what else to do, you were being so stubborn. You were all but accusing me of harassing you, and you were calling my name in your sleep, so I felt like I had to do something. I didn't know how else to get you to believe me."

"Why? Why did you have to do this? Who cares if I sleep-talk, even if it is about you! That's an accident, I don't know why I'm dreaming about you, it just started, it's just…I don't know what it is, but it's not a big deal. Believe me."

"Then why deny it so much? Why not just laugh it off?"

"It was embarrassing."

"I would have understood. I told you, it keeps me up at night. I know about sleep problems. I know how difficult it can be. But you know, for the last night or two, it kept me awake for completely different reasons."

"Because you wanted to tape me and prove you were right."

"In part. But also because you're turning me on, to be honest. I kind of like being in your dreams."

He thought a little flirting might help, but saw the disbelief and fury flash in her eyes. He took a step back as she took a step forward. *Bad move, Raphael.*

"How dare you?" she shrieked, then she turned

and stomped away from him, her shoes squeaking from the water, one heel sticking into the lawn and pulling from her foot altogether. She didn't even stop to pick it up. Her bad day was his fault, even if he'd never meant for it to happen that way.

"Dammit," he cursed under his breath. "Joy!" he called out, not wanting to leave things this way. "Hey, come back. Let's talk this out."

She kept walking to her car, grabbed her bag out, and didn't even cast a dirty look in his direction as she marched up the steps and through the front door.

"Well, that went badly," he said, slamming his hand down on the hood and then checking to make sure he hadn't dented Warren's car.

She'd said she hadn't gotten fired, but apparently someone had heard that tape who shouldn't have. He ran a hand over his face. While he'd never anticipated anything like that happening, he did share in the blame. After all, he'd made the tape and left it there, watched her take it to work. He'd guessed either she'd ignore it or listen to it when she got home, but that was no excuse. He'd screwed up big-time.

He had to find a way to make it up to her. He didn't know why, but he couldn't let things stay as they were. When she'd stood there, furious and crying, it had been all he could do not to cross the driveway and take her in his arms, wipe away her tears.

He didn't know why the impulse was so strong— if he felt guilty, if he was really attracted to her, or just responding to her sexy nighttime chat. Either way, he knew he had to try to make things right. Maybe earn another chance with her.

Most of his talents included life-saving techniques of some sort, and he'd never been accused of being the most romantic guy in the world. As he'd learned from the women in his household, when a guy screwed up this badly, comfort was a big necessity. With that thought, he knew exactly what to do.

5

JOY LEFT HER SOAKED, wrinkled blue suit on the bathroom floor. Demoralized by the day and by breaking down in front of Rafe when she'd meant instead to be cool and intimidating, she stood in the shower relishing the feel of the hot water pounding down on her. In spite of the warm weather outside, the sweltering soak was good. Her muscles were more relaxed, and her headache had receded somewhat.

She reassured herself the office gossip would quickly pass. As soon as something new came along, this incident would be forgotten—that was how office environments worked. If she made herself scarce, she'd weather the storm. She wasn't used to being the subject of office gossip because she tried to be professional in every way. She'd always gotten along with everyone, and didn't make a spectacle of herself at parties or public events, and then today she'd done so in spades.

She closed her eyes as the thought triggered an awful reminder: the office Christmas party was next week, the day before they closed for the holiday.

Great. It was like never-ending torture. She always hated the Christmas party; the food was bad, everyone drank too much, and Ken always insisted everyone stay until the end to exchange their gifts.

She hadn't even picked up a gift for her "secret Santa" contribution, and she wasn't sure what to get. She'd pick up a gift certificate to one of the local stores or restaurants. It was a safe, neutral gift that someone might actually use—unlike the sensual massage kit for two that she'd somehow garnered the year before. It still sat boxed up in the closet.

Wrapped in a thick terry robe, she searched the kitchen, realizing she didn't have any ice cream or much junk food around at all, but neither did she want to go to the store, so she settled for a bowl of cereal. Plopping down in front of the television, she clicked through the channels, groaning as Christmas shows, Christmas music, Christmas ads appeared on every single one of them.

It was insanity. Couldn't they broadcast a show that wasn't about Christmas? There were millions of people like her, sane people who didn't celebrate the holiday.

She clicked off the television, opting to read for a while instead. She searched for the romance novel she'd been consuming in bits and chunks for what seemed to be forever, never sitting down with it long enough to get to the end. She needed a happy ending right now and was determined to enjoy the one between the pages.

The room darkened, and as she reached for the light by the side of the sofa, she blinked at the flash of red then green on the wall opposite where she sat. At first she thought it might be a fire engine, but the green flash killed that thought. Walking to her front window, she saw the house across the street blinking and flashing madly, twinkling its Christmas cheer right into her dark windows.

She couldn't escape. It was *everywhere*.

In the blinking red-and-green assault, she saw the shadow of a figure turn up her walk, heading to her porch. She frowned, squinting to see as the figure came closer.

"Unbelievable!" she huffed, sliding away from the window. There was no way she was dealing with this man again—ever.

The anticipated knock came, softly at first, then louder. He rang the bell, once, not giving up.

She stood still, silent, only breathing when he turned and she heard his footsteps walk away.

Her shoulders relaxed and she grabbed her book from the table, trying to escape the flashing lights by retreating to her bedroom. She'd cuddle up in bed and read, away from everyone. She took off her robe and crawled in under the cotton blanket, not bothering with a nightgown.

Relaxing, finally, she settled back to open her

book when some delectable aroma drifted through the window. Her stomach grumbled, clearly not satisfied with her bowl of cereal.

"Joy?"

She heard his voice and clutched the sheet, tugging it up close under her chin. She parted the curtains, peering through the crack—he was right there, right under her window. She turned off the light so he couldn't see her.

"Joy, I know you're in there. I want to talk—to apologize. Will you let me do that?"

She didn't say anything, obsessed with the fact that he was only a few feet away from where she lay stark naked underneath a sheet in her bed, and while she wanted to be angry, her nipples pebbled against the soft fabric, warmth invading the space between her legs at the sound of his voice—this time it wasn't in her dreams.

"What do you want?" she snapped, disturbed at her own physical response. "Go away."

"No, not until you let me apologize correctly. I made you something. Let me bring it over—you can't be going to bed yet, it's only seven."

"I'm tired. I had a hard day, as you know," she said accusingly.

"I know. Don't you even want to know what I made for you?"

She blew out a breath, gathering the sheet up double and yanking the curtain aside. There he was, standing below her window like a beach-boy Romeo with his sexy eyes and ruffled hair. However, he wasn't offering her a serenade or poetry. Her eyes drifted down to the foil-covered dish in his hands.

"What's that?"

So she was curious. It didn't mean anything.

"It's manicotti. Homemade."

"Really? By whom?"

"By me. My mother taught me, and she's been known to acknowledge, though not in public, that it might even be slightly tastier than her own."

She remained silent, not knowing how to respond.

"I made it for you, Joy. I know it's not enough to make up for what happened today, but I hope it's a start. Let me come in? I'll drop it off for you, apologize and leave. Okay?"

The seductive aroma of the pasta was her undoing—her stomach was listening to Rafe even if she didn't want to.

"Okay. I'll meet you on the porch."

No way was she letting him step inside.

She yanked on a pair of jeans she had thrown over a chair and grabbed a tank top, then headed for the door. She could still smell the manicotti. If she were a stronger woman, a less hungry woman, maybe she could have resisted, but she hadn't had homemade manicotti in, well…ever. Her father hadn't had much time to cook, and she followed in his footsteps in that way, too. Taking a deep breath, she opened the door.

She wasn't sure what made her knees weaker— the smell of the food or the image of Rafe standing there in jeans, a white T-shirt that said Little Italy in faded letters and oven mitts up to his elbows as he held out the hot pan. He slanted a charming smile that she found far too sexy, though his eyes communicated nothing but sincerity.

"It's hot. You got somewhere I can put this down?"

So much for not letting him inside.

"Uh, yeah. Here, follow me to the kitchen."

As she walked, she realized she hadn't thrown on a bra in her haste and she covered her chest with her arms, nodding to the butcher block near the stove. She had little counter space and made up for it with added pieces, the butcher block, the small table in the center with two chairs, though she rarely used both.

"You can set it there. It will be okay on the wood."

He did and stripped off the oven mitts as he did so, revealing strong, tanned forearms. All of her hunger signals were getting mixed up—did she want manicotti or the guy who'd made it?

Stop, she ordered herself, shifting from foot to foot as they stared at each other quietly. She knew she was supposed to say something, but she didn't.

"Okay, well, listen. I hope you enjoy it—it freezes well, so when it cools down, you can cut it up into portions and have dinner for a month. I just wanted to say I'm sorry—about the tape, and the hose, uh, mistake. I didn't mean any harm, and you know, I'll leave you alone now," he said with an air of finality and turned toward the doorway, grabbing his mitts as he went.

She stepped forward, unsure why, but words were coming out of her mouth before she could stop them. "Um, this is an awful lot of food—have you had dinner?"

He turned, his smile brighter, his eyes more hopeful. Dammit. He had gorgeous eyes, a velvet-brown that drew her in, fringed with the long, thick lashes men were so often unfairly graced with.

"Thanks—I am starving, but I wanted this to be a gift. You sure you want to share?"

He was offering her an out. But he had made her a nice dinner, and she'd invited him. So they'd share some food, make nice conversation, and her day would end on a better note than it had started.

"Yes, please, let me get the plates, and you can serve. I don't have any fancy kitchenware, but what I've got is in the drawer there," she babbled, pointing and then turning away in order to compose herself while she got some plates. She rarely had guests for dinner, meeting people out in restaurants instead.

"As long as we can lift out a few pieces, I think that's the basic requirement. My mom says the TV cooking shows have been great for gadget sales, but they make people think that working in a kitchen is more complicated than it needs to be."

She smiled, her spirit lightening as she reached into the cupboard.

"I know," she added, taking out two plates. "Same with the organizational experts—you know, the people who go on the morning shows and clean up someone's messy office by stacking all kinds of new bins and baskets and labeling everything? Like that does any good," she said as she turned back to where he carefully lifted the manicotti from the pan.

Her mouth literally watered while she watched the cheese stretch as he put a large helping on a plate.

"Exactly," he agreed.

The heady aroma nearly brought her to her knees, and she blanked her mind when she started to calculate calories. Fat content be damned.

"If people aren't organized in the first place, adding more buckets and shelves for them to put stuff in will only make the initial problems worse in the long run," he continued.

She stood holding both plates of manicotti, staring at him as if she was seeing him for the first time. Not as the guy who was bugging her about sleep-talking, not as the erotic lover of her dreams, and not as the idiot who'd almost gotten her in deep trouble at work.

She saw a nice, handsome guy with whom she was actually comfortable for more than five minutes at a time. Someone who didn't act as if she had to prove her worth or meet some invisible expectation. Someone who'd brought her dinner. Who had *made* her dinner.

"Are you okay?" he asked, breaking her out of her fugue. "Let me take those, they have to be getting heavy—you want to sit down in the other room or here?"

She blinked as he took the plates. "Here at the table is good. That smells so good I could cry," she said sincerely and then caught his eye as he put the plates down. His face had become far more serious suddenly, and the atmosphere shifted between them.

"I don't want to make you cry again, that's for sure, Joy. I couldn't be sorrier about the first time."

He sat, indicating that he wanted her to start first, his hands at his sides as she took a bite and closed her eyes in bliss.

"Let's not talk about that. This is so good I can't even begin to tell you."

He grinned. "Thanks. Mom would be pleased. Well, maybe not that I helped screw up your day, but that her cooking lessons worked."

"She must be a fabulous cook."

"Straight from heaven," he agreed, digging in to his own dinner.

"Are you an only child?"

"Nope, three sisters, and Mom insisted we all

learn to cook, and Dad insisted we all know our way around a toolbox and a car engine."

"Sounds like a great family."

"I love them, but I'm biased," he said, grinning.

She set her fork down, taking a breather and reaching for her glass of water, frowning as she looked at it. "You know, I think I have some wine in the other room—I'll get it. It was a gift, and I haven't had a chance to open it. Food this delicious deserves more than water to accompany it."

"Sounds good," he added, smiling as she stood to leave the room.

She walked away, weirdly light in her step—after such a terrible, horrible day, she was almost… happy. Reaching to retrieve the wine from the top of the cabinet where she'd set it six months before—she didn't often drink by herself—she didn't question why she was so happy, and returned to the kitchen, stopping short of the table.

"Oh…damn."

"What?"

"I don't have a corkscrew."

"No problem—do you have a toolbox?"

She eyed him warily. "Uh, sure. My dad gave me one when I bought the house."

"Nice thinking. Grab it and we'll have this open in a jiff."

She did and came back to watch him poise a pointy-looking tool over the cork, aiming with the hammer over the wooden handle. He smiled at her, full of mischief, and her heart somersaulted, just a little.

"Move back—in case I miss."

"Maybe we shouldn't—"

Before she could object, he'd brought the hammer down in three expert taps, never missing a beat, and she watched as he pushed the cork down into the wine, drew back and gently levered the sharp point of the tool from the floating cork. Then they were back at the table, finishing their meal and drinking a spicy pinot noir that had only a few bits of cork floating in the bottle.

"Rafe," she started, sitting back in her chair, stuffed and not sure how to broach the conversation. He looked at her curiously, but didn't speak, taking a sip from his glass. The memory of what his mouth felt like—in her dreams, anyway—made her lose her breath for a moment. What was going on?

She never reacted this way to men, even to men she liked. Joy never got the jitters, the quivers and goose bumps other women talked about—in fact, she didn't experience many of the things with men that other women talked about. It was her nature, and she'd come to accept it, but Rafe was throwing her off.

"I really appreciate this—the food and the company, and the apology, though you know, I've been superstressed at work lately. It wasn't your fault, not really—I don't know what possessed me to listen to that disk in the middle of the main office. I guess I didn't think, and that's my fault, not yours."

His eyes darkened. "I'm sorry for my part in it anyway. Are you in serious trouble?"

She shrugged. "I managed to save it at the last minute. I came up with an explanation that was more or less true, sorta." She smiled a little, and he smiled back. "I'm up for a promotion, and I don't know if it's going to happen. I deserve it, I've worked hard for it, but I've been so tired lately, and it's been hard keeping up with everything that's landing on my desk."

"What do you do?"

"Public relations for Carr Toys."

"Cool! You work for a toy company?"

"Yeah, I thought it would be cool, too. It's not. Carr is just another big business trying to make its bottom line. There are some really interesting departments, like the toy design or marketing, but my work involves a lot of pressure, arguing and such."

"How so?"

"I handle toy recalls and company-image issues. You know, like now, with the Toddler Tank, the truck?"

"I saw that story in the paper—that's you?"

"Well, yeah, I'm the lead on customer relations and media communications. It's been a disaster, the wheels falling off of the truck that every little boy wants for Christmas, wheels that present a potential choking hazard. Parents hate Carr toys, and I have to somehow make them happy—the parents and the company."

"That doesn't sound fun," he admitted with a frown. "I never really thought about what happened on the company end of one of those recalls."

"You mentioned you're an EMT, like for the fire department?" she asked, taking the focus away from herself. The wine was making her warm. She studied the slight sheen of perspiration on Rafe's brow, finding it sexy, and licked her lips unconsciously, the taste of wine and sauce still lingering there. She wondered if he tasted as he did in her dreams....

"Yeah, in New York City, for a hospital, not the NYFD. Best city in the world, no offense." He grinned again. "But the insomnia has been dogging me for months—I finally had to take a leave of absence when I almost crashed my ambulance. So, here I am, trying to get over it. Thought a vacation somewhere new, away from the job, might help."

She groaned. "Only to find a loud woman next door keeping you up all night...I'm so sorry. I wish there was something I could do about it. I keep having these dreams," she said emphatically and then remembered whom she was talking to— and exactly whom she was dreaming about—and stopped short.

"When did they start?" he prompted softly, but

the mood changed between them, crackling with sexual tension. She swallowed hard.

"I was having them for a while, but they were just fuzzy, indistinct, frustrating…. Then when you moved in, I saw you…. Suddenly they were about you. I don't know why."

He nodded, and her face turned even hotter, though it wasn't the wine anymore. She was incredibly embarrassed at what she was revealing—the wine was loosening her tongue a little too much, and she pushed the glass away.

"Hey, don't be embarrassed. I'm flattered, personally speaking, but on the other hand, somniloquy is a real sleep disorder."

"Som—what?"

"Somniloquy—talking in your sleep. I know what hell a sleepless night can be. Are you having any other problems, lost sleep, etcetera?"

She wanted to kiss him for understanding—or maybe she just wanted to kiss him, period—and nodded emphatically. "Yes, I'm exhausted. I sleep all night, or seem to, but I am dead tired in the morning."

"Your body is sleeping but your mind isn't—you're probably waking up more frequently than you realize, and lack of sleep will catch up with you."

"You know a lot about sleep."

"That's what happens when you don't get much of it—I've been through the grinder trying to solve my own disorder."

He was being so kind, and that he understood and was so sympathetic made everything far too intimate between them for some reason. She stood and took their plates to the sink, needing to get up and put some distance between them, but it didn't work. He stood and followed her with the remainder of the table's contents.

"Have you tried a sleep clinic, or taking pills?"

She grimaced, leaning against the sink. "I don't think pills will help me stop dreaming about you." She clapped a hand over her mouth too late, sputtering, "I mean, uh…"

He chuckled, reaching past her to turn on the faucet, filling the sink with soapy water. He was way too close, she observed, inhaling his masculine scent, but she didn't move away.

"I know what you mean," he said, leaning against the sink, facing her. "I guess the question is what can you—or we—do about it?"

RAFE WATCHED THE ROSES bloom in her cheeks again. He was fascinated with every little thing about this woman and far too turned on. He shifted slightly, crossing his legs casually and hoping he could mask the hard evidence of his interest as they stood contemplating each other by the sink.

"Joy?" he prompted as she managed to look everywhere around the kitchen but at him.

She stepped away from the counter briskly,

wiping her hands on a towel even though they hadn't actually done any of the dishes. Her expression and her smile were overly bright.

"Hey, thanks for the manicotti. Maybe you should take some home? It's a lot of food for one person."

Suddenly he wasn't aroused, but plenty confused.

"Am I being dismissed then?"

He knew he sounded ticked off and regretted it as he saw the flare of panic in her gaze. She set her hands on her hips, facing him.

"Listen, I don't want you getting the wrong idea—and I think you were."

He crossed his arms over his chest. "What wrong idea would that be?"

He didn't say another word and watched her wrestle with her own discomfort, trying to answer his question without answering it. She mumbled something and he leaned in. "Excuse me? Didn't quite catch that."

She glared at him. "I didn't want you thinking that I was coming on to you—you know, with the dream thing. They're only dreams. That's all."

It made him itch to find a way to show her how prim and proper she wasn't. Whether it was coming out in her dreams or not, he glimpsed the passionate woman who lived beneath the uptight facade. For some reason, beyond his own denied libido, he wanted to bring her out.

"Joy, maybe you need to loosen up. I know you

take your work seriously, and you have a lot of stress, but do you ever have any fun?"

She looked up, frowning. She hadn't expected that, he could tell.

"Of course I do. I have plenty of fun."

"Doing what?"

"I like to read and watch TV, when I'm not working. Sometimes I go to a movie, or go out. Walk on the beach."

"Do you do those things often?"

"When I can, like most people. Work takes up a lot of my time. You don't get promotions by working forty hours a week."

"You sound like you're good at your work, but sometimes people get too wrapped up in their work. I love being an EMT, but it's my job, not my life. I think knowing that is what allowed me to be good at it. Do you love PR?"

"You don't have to love your work to be good at it. I love being good at it."

"Why would you do something that doesn't make you happy?"

Her eyes widened. "Uh, because we're adults and we work, we pay bills, and do what's expected of us. Keeping my house makes me happy."

He blinked—the way she'd said it sounded like someone else talking, not her. He wondered where someone got the concept of work that Joy obviously clung to so strongly.

"Well, that's true, but you can be happy in the meantime."

She shoved her fingers through her hair, and he found himself wondering how soft those strands were.

She yawned. "I'm sorry, I'm tired. It's been a tough day and I have to be up early. Not all of us are on vacation, able to stay up to all hours debating the nature of life and happiness," she said sarcastically but without bite.

"Listen, I have an idea," he said, deciding to ignore the fact that she was withdrawing from him again.

"Does it include walking toward the door?"

He grinned, liking her smart-ass side, even if it was being directed at him at the moment.

"Eventually. You know, if you go to bed now you're only going to be screaming my name in an hour or so," he said teasingly.

"That's not funny."

"No, it's not, but I know a little something about sleep disorders, and maybe yours is caused by all this stress."

Her eyebrow quirked up in the sexiest way he'd ever observed. "Oh, and I suppose you'd like to help me relax?"

He took a step closer, close enough to catch the scent of her soap and shampoo. Her eyes widened, but she didn't look away as he responded.

"Yeah, actually. I'd like that. I have time, I like

you. I think you like me, even if you won't admit it. We could have some fun."

"Exactly what kind of fun are you talking about?"

He didn't bother hiding his attraction as he spoke. "Anything you'd be open to."

"So you did all this, tonight, just to come on to me," she accused, but he shook his head.

"No, I didn't. I promise. I'm honest enough with myself to know that I'm attracted to you—how could I not be? Look at you," he said. "You're a beautiful woman."

"Give me a break," she huffed.

"I'm serious—I haven't been able to get your hair out of my mind since I saw you by the car with the groceries, how you had it all wrapped up tight. Even now, it's pinned back, when you're here alone, at home. Don't you ever want to let it down?"

He tugged a random strand and it fell forward across her ear. He rubbed it between his fingers, and he went hard again. Her gaze was fixed on his, and her lips parted.

"I—I like my hair like this. It's out of my face," she said, her voice catching as she tucked the rogue strand back behind her ear.

He smiled. She wasn't unaffected by him, and that gave him the signal to push a little harder. He wanted her. Maybe it was her dreams that stoked his imagination, but he wanted to loosen her up.

"Joy," he said softly, moving a little closer. "Just let go for a minute."

Before she could stop him, he had tugged off the band that held her hair back, and watched the silky sheet of auburn fall forward, sweeping across her cheek, then back to settle along the gentle curve of her chin. He was entranced with the motion, and touched her hair again.

"Rafe." Her tone held objection, but she didn't step away.

Instead, she closed her eyes, as if she couldn't bear to watch as he slid the palm of his hand underneath the curtain of her hair and curled his fingers around the nape of her neck, pressing slightly before threading back out through her soft tresses. The strands felt like fine ribbons, and he swallowed hard, his hand trembling.

"It's like silk, or softer, actually," he said.

She hadn't opened her eyes, and he took advantage of the moment. He leaned in, stealing a kiss. She startled, and he murmured something, sounds, reassuring her. He darted his tongue out to taste her closed lips, asking for passage beyond. When she opened her mouth, he misinterpreted and took the plunge, moving in for a deeper taste, groaning as he drew her closer, only to find her hands planted between them pushing him back.

"Rafe, no…please." She was breathless, flushed, and it took a minute for his pulse to settle, her words cutting through the fog of passion that had enveloped him so quickly he was amazed.

"I'm sorry," he said, dropping his hands but not stepping back. He looked deep into the blue depths of her eyes. "What's wrong?"

The stiff mask she wore for the world slid back into place, and she wrapped her arms around her middle as if she were cold.

"I was trying to—I was going to say, you have to understand...this won't work. It shouldn't happen."

"Why not?"

He followed her gaze outside the kitchen window toward where the lights strung on Bessie's house blinked and twinkled merrily. The sight still seemed odd to him in the summerlike weather. Finally, Joy spoke, though she kept looking out the window, instead of at him.

"Because I don't like it."

"What? Kissing?"

"No. That...the lights. The decorations, the music, the gifts. Christmas."

"You don't like Christmas?"

"No, I don't."

He frowned. "Okay. Well, I don't think you're alone in that, but what does it have to do with us getting together?"

She aimed a cool, direct gaze at him. "It has to do with us because I don't feel any of it. I'm annoyed by all the clutter and the lights—all of it. As you observed, I hardly know my neighbors, and they don't know me. I don't like my job, particularly, but I like what it gets me. I don't do presents or cookies or carols, and I'm not really into casual sex, either, or sex in general, so you're barking up the wrong tree, okay? I'm not that type of woman."

She'd traveled a long distance in that little monologue, and while he didn't quite get the bit about her not liking Christmas, or why that mattered, the latter comment caught his attention.

"Why would you say you're not the type of woman who enjoys sex?"

She shrugged, trying to look nonchalant, but he could see the burden of past pain in her deliberately calm gaze.

"Believe me, I've gotten feedback on the issue, and I'm just not very…warm. I'm not a warm person."

"You're right," he agreed, garnering a flash of surprised hurt from her before adding, "You're not warm—you're *hot.* Everything about you is hot, and you've got me hot, as well. I hear you at night, and—"

"Those are *dreams,* Rafe—they're not *me.*"

"It is you. Maybe it's the real you trying to get out. Have you ever considered that?"

She looked absolutely miserable at the possibility, and he took a chance, moving closer to her again.

"Listen, Joy, I don't know why you have the picture of yourself that you do, and I agree, you've closed yourself off from some things in life—no, let me finish—I'm not criticizing, and I don't want to be your shrink. You have reasons for what you do and how you do it, and I'm not really about changing that. You're losing sleep, so am I. I'm here for a few weeks, and I like you. I think you might like me. Maybe we can have a little fun together."

"You mean sex."

"I mean fun. If that includes sex, great. I'd love the chance to show you how hot you are. How you affect me," he said honestly. That she could even believe she was a cold fish was beyond him.

"Thanks, but I don't need you to save me," she said stubbornly. He could have been offended, but instead he looked straight back at her, and while he didn't know where the words came from, he knew they were true.

"Who knows? Maybe I need you to save me."

6

"HEY—GOOD WORK TODAY," Ken said, popping his head in the office door and grinning. Joy had been up to her ears regarding the last-minute release of a new and improved Toddler Tank, which was being shipped out to families with recall certificates that very day, a full seven days before Christmas. Manufacturing had done triple-time fixing the problem, and the tide of negative feedback was starting to turn. It was costing the company a fortune, but it would pay off in the long run. Joy had been all over the media all day, making sure everyone knew what a good job her company had done.

"Thanks." She took the time to look up and smile back at Ken.

"Um, how's that other thing going—you know, with the problem you were having, whoever's leaving you those, uh, materials?"

She blushed, his comment taking a little of the shine off the moment. "It's fine—I made sure it was addressed last night," she said.

The relief on Ken's face was palpable. No doubt

he was glad he didn't have to deal with it internally. "That's good. Well, you really stayed on top of things today. I was impressed."

All was forgiven, and everyone was in a great mood with the great save they'd managed to make. This aspect of the job was much more gratifying than all the negativity she'd been wading through before.

"You've been at it all day—it's six—you heading out soon? I thought I could buy you a congratulations drink," Ken proposed.

"Six? Oh, crap—sorry, I mean, thanks for the offer on the drink, but can I take a rain check? I have somewhere to be, and I lost track of time."

"Hot date?"

Ken was happily married, so she knew he wasn't coming on to her. "No, volunteer work I do in the evenings."

"You're a wonder, Joy. Not everyone would work all day and then volunteer at night. Make sure that's noted on your employee profile."

"That's not necessary. It's something I do because I enjoy it."

"Still, can't hurt to keep building that résumé. Joy?"

"Yes?"

"You really did a great job on this recall—I'll be sure to make that known to the board when we're making the promotion decisions."

She smiled, nodding. "Thanks, Ken, I appreciate that."

She practically danced to the parking lot—she was back on track, and in line for the promotion. At the moment, she had to grab some dinner and get to Second Chance. She'd offered to do the night shift there and had her change of clothes in the backseat, ready to go.

When Pam had called that morning asking her to cover at the last minute because Rashid couldn't make it, she'd jumped at the chance, maybe a little too eagerly. There was the small—teensy, really— chance that she was avoiding going home since Rafe might be tempted to come over and see her. The events of the previous evening had been thrumming through her brain and her body all day long, and she didn't know what to think about it, except that she didn't want to think about it.

However, Rafe had been wrong about one thing: she hadn't gone to sleep and dreamed about him because she'd been up, tossing and turning and trying not to think about how he'd tenderly touched her face, the heat in his gaze, or the gentle kiss he'd offered—with the promise of so much more.

If she'd dared let herself fall asleep she would have spontaneously combusted, having been so close to him, his presence following her into sleep. So she'd stayed awake, his words echoing in her mind as she realized she didn't need to go to sleep to have Rafe Moore—he was offering himself to her on a silver platter. Maybe she was crazy, but it scared her to death.

In her dreams she was a different woman, unin-
hibited, sensual—not her ordinary, uptight self. She
meant what she'd told him—she dated, sure, and
she'd liked a few of the guys she'd seen over the
years well enough to take things to their inevitable
conclusion in the bedroom. She'd dealt with the
sting of more than one breakup, as well. None of the
men had said she was awful in bed or anything, but
what else was a girl to think? She obviously didn't
have the sex appeal she did in her dreams. Dream
sex was usually more satisfying for her, too, sadly.
Even so, she hoped it would cease soon—her sleep
deprivation was wearing her out.

Rafe was interested in her because he'd heard
that sexy version of herself, not the real Joy. Joy was
willing but awkward, generally not knowing exactly
how to respond to a man's touch. She didn't want
to be like that, but even when she wanted to partici-
pate, she never felt natural or carried away by
passion. It was a self-perpetuating problem that had
converted a rather boring sex life into a bona fide
dry spell. Rafe was offering to help her end it, but
his interest was based on false information.

That was why she'd pushed him away—he had
a fantasy of her and it was so far from reality that
it could only lead to disappointment for both of
them. Rafe might like her hair down, but it would
take a lot more than freeing her hair to thaw out
whatever made her so boring in bed. The one thing

she was sure of was that she couldn't face seeing disappointment in her performance mirrored in yet another man's eyes.

Especially not in Rafe's hot-chocolate eyes.

She hoped he'd take the hint and back off. Better to nip this in the bud, she thought as she drove into the Second Chance parking lot.

Cheery multicultural holiday decorations were on display in the windows and on the lawn. People who stayed at the shelter came from varied backgrounds. There was a menorah in the window circled by Christmas lights. A Santa stood on the small scruffy patch of front lawn beside a makeshift manger. Joy smiled, realizing this was the only time looking at all the Christmas decorations hadn't made her wrinkle her nose.

Maybe it was because here the decorations meant something more than the suburban competition to outdo one's neighbors. Here, this little pastiche of holiday cheer represented hope…and home, if only for the moment. For people who lived here and were working so hard to improve their lives, this was a sign of their belief in something good. Bolstered, she got out of the car. She was avoiding Rafe, but even that couldn't dim her optimism as she walked through the doorway, looking forward to her evening.

"WOW—LOOK AT YOU!"

Pam spun around, surprised. She hadn't even

heard Joy walk up. She also wasn't decked out in her usual jeans, T-shirt and Padres cap with a pen stuck behind her ear.

"This looks okay?" Pam asked hesitantly, smoothing the sides of her deep green formfitting dress down for what must have been the fiftieth time, flashing looks in the mirror and then at Joy for reassurance. Pam's fortysomething curves were still holding up, and she didn't look half-bad, but she hadn't dressed up like this in such a long time. She just wasn't sure.

"Okay? You look amazing. I love your hair that way—that pretty little holly clip is a nice touch. That dress is to die for. I don't think I've ever seen you this dressed up—or this nervous."

Pam smoothed her dress yet again. "I have a date, but I'm thinking twice about it."

"Is this about your mystery man? You know, I promised not to push, but if he has you this nervous, he must be terrific, or is something wrong?" Joy prompted.

Pam knew she wasn't being fair, keeping her relationship a secret. Besides, tonight everything would be out in the open anyway, so she certainly should tell Joy, whom she considered her best friend. She was so afraid of recriminations, especially since Joy meant so much to her. What if when Pam told her, Joy thought she was a total skank? Still, she had to take that chance.

"He is…terrific. This is our first dress-up date, and I don't know. I had this event, a Christmas party with the local chamber of commerce, you know, because of all the business connections I have with the shelter, and so I go every year, and this time I thought, well, maybe I won't go alone. So I asked him."

Joy nodded approvingly. "Sounds like a good plan. But. Who. Is. He?" Joy insisted playfully, and Pam bit her lip, drawing up the courage to answer her question.

"It's Ted."

"Ted?" Joy repeated, her brow furrowed. Then her eyes went wide with realization. "*Our* Ted? Ted Ramsey?"

"Yeah, that's the one," Pam said, tensing as she mentally braced herself.

"Wow. I can see that—I mean, I didn't see it, but now it seems so obvious. You guys would be great together. How long have you two been, you know…?"

Pam sagged against the desk. "We had an immediate attraction—I knew it shouldn't happen, but we gave in after he'd been staying here about six months."

"You and Ted have been together for almost two years and no one knows? This is your first dress-up date?"

"Well, we were on and off—some long off periods while he got his life back on track, and we both knew it was against the rules. Can you imagine how it would look if anyone knew I was sleeping with one of our residents?"

"I guess I can see where you'd be concerned, but it's not like he's a child, or incapable of making his own decisions, Pam. You're two adults who are attracted to each other. What's wrong with that?"

Pam's eyes shone with tears and she tried to dab at them before she ruined her makeup, but she was losing the battle. "I was so worried you'd think I'd crossed the line," Pam said, sighing with relief.

"It sounds like you've been keeping it in for so long, you probably just let it build up in your mind—why would anyone care?"

"I run this place, and I love it. It's my life. The people who come here are adults, yes, and they have to take responsibility for their lives, but they're also disadvantaged with the odds against them, and I wouldn't want anyone thinking I took advantage or, you know, that anything…unsavory was going on here."

Pam tried to find words, but her face simply flamed hot. "I tried to stick to the rules, we both did. Flirtatious or sexual behavior here is very strictly prohibited for good reasons, as you know. But it was like every time we saw each other, or spoke to each other, we couldn't think about the rules."

Joy smiled a little. "You want my honest opinion?"

Pam nodded.

"I think it's really romantic. Ted's a great guy—

he was what? Around thirty-nine when he came here? He'd had a tough break that nearly ruined his life, but he didn't let it, and you helped him make it the rest of the way—but look at him now. I'm surprised I never saw it before. It makes total sense, since you spend most of your time here anyway. It's no different than meeting someone at work."

"I suppose," Pam agreed tentatively.

"He's been so happy. I guess I figured it was natural for him to be so jovial. He's gotten his life back together and he's almost completed his college degree—but I think you're the one who put the sparkle in his eyes."

Joy laughed and Pam blushed again, though she was also pleased that Joy hadn't reacted badly.

"Thanks. I can't tell you what a load off it is to be able to tell you."

"I was wondering what was going on, I have to be honest. I thought maybe you didn't trust me or something."

"How could you think that?" Pam was shocked. "I trust you completely. This was… Well, I don't know. I didn't know what to say. Ted and I swore we wouldn't tell anyone until we were both ready."

"So how come it took you so long to go out on a real date? I mean, I can understand why you'd want to keep things under wraps, but you could have gone out long before this, couldn't you?"

"Oh, we do, we go out all the time, but just the

two of us. But those were small, private dates, nothing fancy. Nothing with other people. You know, where people would know us."

"So that's what you're nervous about?"

"I don't know." Pam looked in the small mirror she had hanging over her desk, grabbing a tissue to fix her slightly smudged makeup. "I guess I'm worried what people will say."

"Like your parents? Do they know?"

Pam rolled her eyes. "No. Haven't hit that hurdle yet, but they're bound to have a coronary. After I rejected all the 'eligible' bachelors they wanted me to marry for all those years, I think they finally assumed I was probably gay, and were happy not to know if that was the case or not."

"I never understood why they don't support this cause—their picture is in the paper often enough in connection to other charity events."

"It's hard to explain. That's when they can donate large checks, not get their hands dirty. They wouldn't mind if I supported causes, they don't approve of my level of…involvement."

"I'd think they'd be proud of you."

"Well, we've maintained a truce about it over the years, since they could see I wasn't about to stop my work. My relationship with Ted will be the real test. I can't allow anything to threaten this place—we're already struggling enough. A harsh blow like someone saying I act inappropriately could be a disaster."

"I guess I can see that, though this is personal—it never interfered with the work you do, so it's really no one's business."

"Well, we'll see. Tonight is our first public event together. Ted wanted to wait until he was out on his own, and he's almost completely moved into the new place. We're going to move in together after the New Year."

"How wonderful!" Joy crossed the room and gave her a congratulatory hug, and Pam smiled, her happiness at the prospect shining through her concerns.

"Yeah, and he's been really instrumental in coming up with some good business strategies for Second Chance. He's as devoted to it as I am, you know, and I guess, I don't know…"

Pam was relieved when Joy seemed to read her mind.

"You don't know if you want that? This place is yours, and now you find you're sharing your whole life, including the shelter?"

"It's mostly that, yes, but I also want him to have his own thing."

"I can see what you mean, though. You've built this place. It is yours, but I can also see why he'd want to be involved, and use his talents to help you out."

"I want to make sure that he follows his own goals. He's worked hard to be where he is, and maybe he should go after his MBA or start his own business or do something…I can't quite figure out if this is really what he wants, or if he's only being…grateful."

"Even if he is, is there something wrong with that? I think it's sweet that he wants to be part of your life, and to help out. Ted hardly seems like the type not to go after what he wants—after all, he got you," Joy teased.

"There's a good point." Pam smiled, shaking her head. "I don't know—meeting here muddied the waters, I guess. We knew who we were when he was here, but now, well, some of the rules have changed. We're into a new stage of our relationship. I don't know how to separate it all out."

"You love him."

"Yeah, I do."

"Then you'll work it out."

"You're right, we will. Thanks. So how about you?"

"What about me?"

"Any news about the hottie next door?"

"Oh. I can't believe I forgot this—or I suppose I should thank you for helping me forget it, at least for a little while," Joy groused.

Pam listened to Joy's story about the tape, so engrossed that she forgot her own troubles.

"Oh, honey—that's terrible. Sounds like he made up for it, though."

"Yeah, he did, but I'm so foggy from not getting any sleep I can't seem to tell left from right anymore."

"Well," Pam said slyly, "I think we discussed that the solution to your sleep problem might be right next door."

"He said the same thing," Joy said, sighing.

"Okay, I have to go, so make this fast—what happened? Don't edit," she warned.

Pam was intrigued. She'd wished for Joy to meet someone wonderful for so long, and now it sounded as if she'd met someone truly different from the boring corporate types she usually dated. Maybe it was true that people in love wanted all their friends in relationships, too, but Pam truly wanted to see Joy happy. She worked hard and was a devoted friend. Over the years though, Pam had come to see that Joy held something back in her life. There was something deep inside she kept locked up, and Pam had always hoped the right man might come along with a key.

"After dinner, things got a little…heated. He kissed me, he said he wanted more, maybe."

"So what's the problem? He's cute, and you're available—go for it."

"Go for it? Of course I can't go for it—he's just some guy who's in town for a few weeks looking for some action."

Pam tilted her head to the side. "Yes? Exactly what do you see wrong with that scenario? A fling is ideal—you have some fun, don't take it all so seriously. You don't have to worry if this guy meets anyone's standards but your own—he's temporary. It's not like you'd be bringing him home to meet your parents."

Joy frowned, perplexed. "I guess I figure when I get involved with someone, it's for the long term, and I do tend to measure men by what my dad would think of them. I think that's natural. He raised me."

"You measure everything that way, Joy, and while your father is a good guy, maybe you need to start measuring things with your own stick. Including yourself. What do you want? What makes you happy?"

Joy frowned. "I—I'm not sure. I thought I was happy. I guess I haven't thought about it much."

"Well, think about it. Some rules are meant to be broken. Believe me, I know." Pam smiled.

"Speaking of which, when's Ted getting here?" Joy asked, not so subtly changing the subject.

"He's not—no one here knows about us yet, and I don't think they should until he's no longer living here, so we're meeting at the party."

"It must be hard, keeping it secret."

"It has been, especially from you—but I care about your opinion, and I was so afraid you would disapprove."

"Why would I? I love you and Ted."

"I know. I wish I'd told you sooner, but we thought it was better this way."

"That's fine. It probably added that whole forbidden-lust factor, huh?" Joy teased, laughing as Pam's cheeks stained red again.

"You're bad. Anyway, thanks for standing watch tonight."

"No problem."

As they walked out to the main room, Pam took a few bows and curtsies as she received compliments on her dress. Both women were surprised when Rashid, the night-shift staff, came in the front door.

"Rashid! I thought you weren't able to be here tonight?" Pam asked.

"I had my schedule wrong—I'm due at the warehouse tomorrow night, so I'm good for tonight. Sorry if it messed you up," Rashid said.

"I don't know how you do it all, Ras," Pam commented and Joy echoed the sentiment. Rashid ran the teen shelter across town and also worked a third shift in a home-improvement supply warehouse, on top of finishing his grad degree in social work. He'd spent his childhood on the streets, and Pam respected how he'd changed his life through sheer determination to do so. Growing up in the privileged environment that she had, where everything came so easily, she found it inspiring to know the people she did.

"If you still want the night off, Rashid, I'll stay. I was prepared to, anyway," Joy offered.

Rashid shook his head. "Thanks, but I'm good. I want to talk with some of the guys tonight."

Pam looked at Joy, grinning. "I guess that means

you get to go home early. Maybe check in on your neighbor, see what he's cooking tonight."

Joy glared, and Pam laughed, her friend's excuse to avoid her neighbor flying right out the window.

7

RAFE HUNG UP THE PHONE, deflated and lonely. First he'd called his parents, who were missing him, and his mother had done a primo job trying to get him back home for Christmas. It was hard for them to understand why he wanted to be so far away, that he needed to be far away from the job. If he was back in the city, all he'd be able to think about was work, and that wouldn't help him.

Of course, then he'd returned a call from Steve, the guy he'd been riding the ambulance with for the last three years. Steve's wife had just given birth to their second child, and Steve had called to share the good news. Rafe was happy for his bud, but the conversation inevitably had turned to work.

Rafe missed it the way he would miss one of his limbs. He'd started college thinking he wanted to be a doctor. In his junior year he'd volunteered as an EMT and was hooked. He'd worked his way up to being a registered paramedic, and he loved it. The rush, the speed, the immediacy of helping people when they most needed it—it all made his blood run and his heart beat.

Until he'd started having nightmares and losing sleep. Gradually, he'd found he was getting frazzled, not handling the stress as well, not processing the emotions that came with the job. Classic burnout, his colleagues had told him—it got everyone eventually, and he'd lasted longer than many.

He'd thought he could handle it, thought it would pass on its own, but when he'd realized his pride could have cost Steve's kids a father the night he'd nearly crashed the ambulance, Rafe knew he couldn't keep going. He couldn't do the job he loved, and he would never be able to do it again if he couldn't solve this problem.

The sleeping pills had side effects that could be as bad as not sleeping, so drugs were not really an option. So here he was, two thousand miles away from everything he knew, staring out Warren's window into a December evening that looked more like the Fourth of July.

Needing some air, he broke away from where he was sitting on the side of the bed and went out the front door, no destination in mind, just needing to get out. Standing out on Warren's front walk, he relaxed his breathing, chasing the stress from his mind as he started working through a series of stretches. The sun dipped and the lights on the houses around him clicked on.

As he leaned over, his eye landed on the single unlit spot on the street. Joy's house. The windows were dark, the car gone, not a creature was stirring in that lonely little house. He'd heard her car leave that morning—before the sun had come up, even though they'd been awake most of the night before. Where could she be now? Working late? Out with friends? Volunteering at the shelter she obviously loved so much? Avoiding him?

Why did he like Joy Clarke so much, exactly? He barely knew her.

Didn't matter; he couldn't keep his mind off her.

Straightening, he looked at the dark facade of her home again and contemplated her dislike of Christmas. She'd said she didn't like it—that the lights annoyed her—but maybe she needed someone to share it all with? He'd asked her to hook up with him, essentially, and she'd shied away. Maybe there was another way to reach her.

Jumping in his car, he made a quick trip to the local home-improvement warehouse. Since he'd been working on Warren's house, the staff recognized him. Several eager young female clerks helped him pick out decorations, and encouraged him when he told them his plan. As he drove home, the more he thought about it, the more determined he became.

Back at Warren's, he grabbed his ladder, brought it over to Joy's yard and got started. He'd have to work fast, as she could be home any second. The more he had done, the harder it would be for her to tell him to undo it. He smiled devilishly to himself.

An hour later, when he was up on the roof and nearly finished, he heard a car's motor and looked down, watching Joy pull into her driveway, stop, then drive forward the rest of the way.

He swung down over the edge back to the ladder and heard her car door slam.

"What the hell are you doing?"

He was prepared for her temper and turned around calmly, greeting her politely.

"Evening, Joy. Putting up some lights—you're the only house on the block without a single light on," he answered, nonplussed. "It's not a lot—a bit around the edge of the roof and corners—you won't even be able to see them from inside."

She glowered. "I don't want to see them at all—you have no right to have your way with my house!"

He couldn't help but grin at her phrasing—her house wasn't the only thing he wanted to have his way with.

"Stop smiling at me like that! I'm serious!" she said between clenched teeth.

"I know you are. I'll make you a deal. You help me finish putting up these lights, and we'll turn them on, and if you still don't like it, I'll take them down. Though I've been working on them for quite a while, so it may have to wait until tomorrow," he said with a sigh.

"It's been a long day, Rafe…."

"All the more reason for you to do something fun at the end of it. With me," he said, bending to hand her a coil of wire and lights. "Hold these and feed them up to me as I clip them, okay? This is the last bunch."

She sputtered for a moment, but he hopped back up the ladder, not giving her a chance to object. Sure enough, she walked to the edge and fed him the lights as he neatly clipped them into place.

"Did you end up working late?" he inquired casually, filling the silence between them.

"No. I went by the shelter."

"Hmm," was all he said, earning another curious look.

"What's that supposed to mean?"

"I thought maybe you were trying to wait me out and come home late, so I might get the hint that you're not interested."

"It didn't work, apparently."

He looked down, catching her eye unabashedly. "That's because I know it's not true. Just like I know you're not going to hate these lights, even though you're going to want to."

"You're pretty cocky for a guy I just met." The comment was dry, but not angry, so he figured he was making progress.

"I have a good sense of people. I had to in my line of work."

"You're wrong about the lights—you're going to end up taking them all down again."

He gave himself a mental high five as he realized she hadn't denied her interest in *him*.

"Could be. Maybe you need to look at having these lights up here from a different perspective," he offered, hanging the final string and making his way back to the ground.

"How so?"

"Plug that in over there, and we'll see."

She shook her head but did go to the corner of the house to plug in the cord. Immediately, her house was outlined in soft white and red lights.

"I liked the red and white—like peppermint," he said, standing back to admire his work.

"I guess. What did you mean, a different perspective?" she asked finally.

"Well, I wanted to do this for you. However, even if you don't enjoy Christmas decorations so much, there's a neighborhood of people here who will. The kids, especially. I used to walk the streets back home and look at all the lights when I was a kid." He was quiet for a moment, letting his words sink in. Joy obviously had a sense of social purpose or she wouldn't volunteer at the shelter. He figured all he had to do was appeal to that part of her.

"Now, when they walk by your house, it will lift their spirits. It makes you part of the neighborhood, part of the community. When Bessie looks out her front window, she'll see your lights the same way you see hers. It'll make her smile, and you know, she needs that. The holidays are difficult for people who've lost loved ones."

He could tell from her quiet contemplation of the lights that he'd made her reconsider. Joy obviously cared about others—maybe more than she cared about herself.

"If you think I can't see how you're being so clever with manipulating me, think again," she said tartly. "I guess they're pretty. It's not too much."

"So they can stay up?"

"Yeah, I suppose."

Cheerful about his victory, he grabbed her and kissed her, not allowing her time to put up her defenses. Instead, much to his surprise, she put her hands around the back of his neck, tentatively at first, and then with more commitment as she opened her lips and let him explore further.

Delighted to comply, he tasted her thoroughly, rubbing his tongue along the contours of hers, teasing every satin inch of her mouth. He eased his arms around her, taking in the graceful sway of her lower back, the curves below, and kept himself busy memorizing every nuance of her mouth.

She sighed against his lips, kissed him back gently, but mostly allowed him to find his way around her, and he didn't mind that one bit. Though when he drew back and gazed at her face, taking in flushed cheeks and her lowered eyelids, he couldn't help but wonder what had changed.

"I guess you really liked the lights more than you thought you would," he said teasingly and saw a hint of a smile at the edge of her well-kissed lips.

"I think I like you a little more than I thought I would," she confessed, surprising him.

Not wanting to let the fires die out, he dipped down, nuzzling the warm skin of her neck. She shivered even though it was far from cold outside.

"I'm glad about that. Want to go inside?"

She hesitated, as if weighing her response, and then nodded. Without a word, she took her keys from her pocket and he could see her hands tremble. Desire or something else?

He followed her in. As the door closed, her keys fell to the carpet along with her bag, and he didn't waste a moment.

"I love how you taste," he shared before devouring her mouth again, urging her to respond, to take him as much as he wanted to take her. He licked the thundering pulse in her throat, knew that she liked it by the soft sigh she couldn't hold back. "Touch me back, Joy. Kiss me back," he said against her mouth.

She did, and when he slid his hands up under her shirt, she moaned into his mouth as his palms closed over her breasts, kneading through the fabric of her bra, teasing her nipples to fine points that he enjoyed playing with.

Rafe pressed his erection against her hip, rubbing gently. He was close, ready to explode. It had been a long while and he was starving for release.

She seemed to notice, intuiting his need to be touched, and slipped her hand down inside his jeans. He caught his breath audibly when her fingers closed around his length and he pressed into her harder. They dove into each other's kisses enthusiastically and within seconds he gave in, groaning as he came, unable to hold back. It was one of the most erotic things he'd ever experienced, so much so that he remained hard, barely finished but ready to go again.

"Uh-oh, we're one-nothing now—want to go to bed early and even the score?" he asked teasingly, weaving his hands through her hair and nuzzling her warm skin.

He could taste the sheen of perspiration that had formed there, turning him on more. This first time had been fast, taking the pressure off, but when he got her upstairs he'd show her that her dreams paled compared to reality. He wanted to make her scream with pleasure while she was completely awake.

"Oh, no, I don't think so. That's all right," she said quickly, extracting her hand and slipping away from him, hitting the light switch by the door.

He blinked in confusion, watching her bend to pick up her keys and coat, putting her keys in her pocket. She smoothed her shirt and hair, as if, well, as if they were done.

"Excuse me?" He walked over and tugged her up against him, looking down into her eyes, her face only inches from him.

The desire he'd experienced with her in the semidark by the door vanished, however, the only hints of it remaining in the color of her cheeks, her swollen lips and the musky smell of sex between them. He could see the stemmed desire in her eyes, the tautness of her features, as if she were under stress. He'd be happy to relieve it for her, but had no idea what she was doing.

"What game are you playing, Joy?" He was still on edge, his body hot for hers and his emotions scrambling. He didn't like how she just shut it off, the passion. It made what had happened, well…cheap.

"No games." She put her hands on his arms, pushed back, getting some physical distance. "I…I don't know why I did that. It was nice, it's okay— you don't have to, ah, even the score. It was a mistake, obviously."

"Why?" He wrapped his arms around her even though she gasped an objection and tried to push away. But he held her there, moving his hands firmly around her back. Her resistance was nominal, as if she were fighting herself more than him. Finally, she looked up at him.

"You're only here for a few weeks. This won't go anywhere. I don't know you."

What he'd interpreted as distance he now

realized was not that at all, but instead closer to fear or anxiety. He loosened his hold, but stayed close.

"So you'll spend a couple weeks getting to know me, and we'll have some fun. Remember fun, Joy? Have you ever really let yourself go and not worried about every little thing?"

"Easy for you to say, you're on vacation, you don't have a career that needs your attention, and you—"

"You said you don't know me—and you're right," he reminded her tersely. "You don't. This isn't completely a vacation, Joy. It's a leave of absence because I couldn't do my job. A job I happen to love, and which has been my whole life. So don't say I don't understand that. Now I can't do it, because I can't get a damned night's sleep."

He stepped back, wiping a hand over his face, lowering his voice when he saw her stunned expression. Great. She'd hit a nerve, and their emotions were running high, but that didn't give him the right to lash out.

"Listen, maybe you're right, I'm sorry—"

She took a step forward. "No… You're right. I don't know you, so I shouldn't make assumptions. I didn't mean to do that, I didn't know…" She drifted off as if searching for the words, and he waited.

"You're right. I haven't had fun in so long…. Maybe that's why my blood pressure's up—"

"You have high blood pressure?" he asked, slipping into his EMT role without a second thought.

She smiled. "Slightly. The doctor wasn't concerned, but she did tell me to find ways to relax more. I guess I didn't really follow that prescription."

He took another chance. "Maybe I could help with that?"

His stomach actually did a little flip when her cheeks turned hot as if merely thinking about having fun excited her, and he experienced the corresponding stir in his lower regions again. They could have a little fun together.

"I don't know, Rafe, I can't make any promises about...*that*." She glanced meaningfully toward the door, and he knew to what she was referring. "I've never been very good with, uh, sex. I don't seem to enjoy it much."

Saying the word made her cheeks burn even hotter and he watched her flailing, wondering how she could think such a thing about herself.

"Coulda fooled me, honey, but a lot of people are insecure about sex and—"

"No, take my word for it—that's why I keep dreaming, like I do—that never happens in real life. Ever. It's never been my...thing." Her hands flew up, covering her red face as she moaned with embarrassment. He pried her fingers away.

"Listen. Part of having fun is no pressure, so there isn't any. There's fun, and then there's *fun,* and I'd like to have both kinds with you, but you lead the way, okay?"

She took a deep breath, obviously relieved, though her hands were ice cold in his. He was going to make it his personal challenge to warm her up.

"Okay. Thanks," she said.

"Who knows?" he said, pulling her against him. "Maybe we'll end up making a few dreams come true."

8

"THIS IS ONE OF THE MOST magical nights of my life," Pam whispered, a delicious shiver running down her spine as Ted's big, powerful hand touched her gently at the spot where the back of her dress scooped down past her shoulder blades.

"Every night is magic since I met you," he responded in the husky drawl that she loved. If they weren't at a business-oriented event, she would have snuggled even closer, thrilled that their first public appearance together was going so well.

Her forty-two-year-old hormones were dancing right along with them. Who knew love and passion would find her at this point in her life? Being with Ted made her feel as if she were twenty again. They couldn't seem to get enough of each other. The flames of desire were licking at her again.

"I wish we could be open about everything so that everyone could admire you as much as I do," she said regretfully, and he squeezed her hand in response.

"It's better that they don't know how we met, for the sake of the shelter, but for me, too, Pam. I don't want people looking at me for where I came from. I want them to see me as I am, now. With you. With my degree in hand, my new place, my new job… The past should be left in the past."

Pam didn't completely agree, if only because Ted had picked himself up from such a low point and had not only defeated the odds, but beat them senseless. She loved him; she was proud of him and she knew his story would give other people hope. Unfortunately, it would also raise suspicion and cast a jaundiced eye on her reputation as a non-profit manager. While they were two consenting adults, they couldn't make their history general knowledge. It was too risky.

They couldn't even have people at the shelter know—it would open too many doors that should stay shut. After a while, when Ted was out on his own, established in his work and his life, they could let everyone know, saying they'd gotten together after the fact.

Still, it bothered Pam so much to have to lie.

The music ended and she didn't realized how tense she'd become in Ted's arms until he looked into her eyes with concern. She blew out a breath, laughing softly.

"Okay, sorry. I know I should leave work at the office." She dropped her hands from his shoulders as they walked from the dance floor. "I love that tux—you look right at home in it."

"Pays to buy quality."

She stepped back in surprise. "You bought that? It's yours?"

He grinned. "I wasn't taking you out in a rented monkey suit, and I plan to get a lot of use out of this over the years. Clothes make the man," he reminded her, a quote from one of their favorite goofy movies, *Joe Versus the Volcano.* She grabbed his hand and tugged him down close.

"No. I think in this case it's very much the opposite."

"Well, thank you ma'am," he said, his eyes sparkling with desire. "How about one more drink, and then we can take the party home?"

"That sounds like a perfect plan," she agreed.

She'd stayed a respectable time, had fun, mingled with the people she needed to mingle with, catching them up on the shelter's latest doings and making sure they knew how critical their donations and services were to the shelter's success. She'd even managed to convince the manager of a small local grocery chain not to drop their program asking customers to donate at the cash register. Every small victory counted.

Glancing toward the bar to see if Ted was making his way back to her, Pam caught the eye of Martin Solese of Solese Construction. She hadn't seen him earlier, and he was one person she was trying desperately to hold on to—the shelter needed new front steps in the worst way and she didn't have enough cash on hand to pay full cost. However, Martin had become so in demand in the local housing market that she never really saw him anymore. His secretary said she forwarded Pam's calls, but Pam never got a response.

She thought it might have to do with the fact that he'd asked her out once and she'd said no, definitively. She didn't mix business with pleasure as a rule, and she'd explained that to him; she hadn't wanted to jeopardize his support by going out with him. She'd also just met Ted at that time and hadn't been interested in anyone else. She pasted on a smile as Martin approached the table.

"Pam! How are you? You look too gorgeous to be here all alone—didn't I see you dancing with someone?"

She nodded as he took a chair close by her side, Ted's chair, wishing he'd taken one a few seats away. "I am here with someone. He's getting drinks now. I didn't see you here earlier."

"Ah, got off to a late start tonight, waiting for my date."

"Anyone I know?"

"Probably not. She's a model from L.A.—we met when I was hired to do a summer house for her father. We've been seeing each other for a few months now." He delivered the news in a tone that subtly suggested that Pam had missed out. If he was serious about someone else, it would make it much easier to ask him to do some work on the shelter.

"Listen, Martin, I wanted to talk to you about some work we need done—"

"Here we are…. Martini for you and, oh…hello," Ted interrupted them, and Pam looked up, glad he had returned.

"Thanks. Oh, Ted, I wanted to introduce you to—"

"Ted… Don't I know you from somewhere?" Martin interrupted, his expression surprised as he stood and shook Ted's hand. Pam noticed that Ted had gone a little pale and set his drink down on the table with a shaking hand.

"No, I don't think so," Ted responded gruffly. And then it hit her and she felt slightly panicked— of course, Martin had been working on installing new windows right at the time Ted had arrived at the shelter. It seemed unlikely that either man would remember the other, so much time had passed.

"I remember," the contractor said, tapping his forehead now, "you helped me put in windows when I did that job at the shelter. Weren't you…you know, uh, weren't you staying there?"

Martin stumbled and Ted caught Pam's eye as the two other couples returned from the dance floor— one of them being the grocer she'd convinced to keep supporting them.

The three stared at each other as the implications struck them all simultaneously. Pam hoped against hope that Martin wouldn't make anything of it. As he turned his narrowed gaze on her, she saw the anger tighten his jaw and she knew she wasn't going to be that lucky.

"So…I asked you out at the time and you said you didn't want to date me because we had a conflict of interest due to my donating work to the shelter—however, it appears that you didn't feel the same conflict of interest in getting involved with one of your charity cases? Is Ted special or do you take care of all your male residents that well?"

Pam recoiled but heard Ted growl from across the table.

"You'd best take that back and apologize, Solese," he warned in a tone of voice she'd only ever heard him use when some of the guys at the shelter got out of line. She looked up to see him towering over Martin.

Mr. Douglas, the grocery-store owner, broke in, confused. "What's going on here Ms. Reynolds? What are these two men fighting about?"

People around them in the country club had started milling about and observing the two men angrily staring each other down. It was too late to save face—the best she could do was to try to keep them from pounding each other.

"Ted, stop—Martin, back off—you're out of line."

Martin laughed, looking around at his audience.

"Oh, I'm out of line? I think you're the one who's out of line, dating your male residents…. How many people here know? What do you think they'd think if they did?"

"That's enough, Martin," she cautioned in her own icy tone, reeling with anger. How *dare* he call her out like this? "I don't owe any explanations to you or anyone. I can date whomever I like. It just so happened not to be you. The conflict of interest was an excuse—I wouldn't have gone out with you anyway, so accept that fact and deal with it."

Every person's eyes were trained on her, including Ted, who had lowered his fists, thank God. Martin was so outraged he was beyond words.

Mr. Douglas broke the silence. "If I am not mistaken, am I to understand that you, Ms. Reynolds, have been dating this man, and he is one of your residents at Second Chance?"

"Yeah, that sums it up nicely," Martin added nastily, and she shot him another glare before turning her attention to Mr. Douglas.

"Mr. Douglas, this is a terrible misunderstanding. Martin is only upset because I turned him down for a date, that's all, and maybe everyone has had a few too many martinis," she offered, trying to lighten the mood, but it wasn't happening.

Douglas was old school, and she knew he already had reservations about Second Chance as it was— he'd heard some news story "exposing" homeless people as con men and layabouts who would rather live off the system than work for a living. It had taken her a while to convince him that that was not the case, at least not in her program.

"Ms. Reynolds, has your date been a resident of your shelter or not?"

"Mr. Douglas, this really is not the place for this discussion. If we could make an appointment to talk in private—"

"I'll happily make that appointment if you can tell me he was *not* one of your residents."

Pam chewed her lip, painfully aware of all the people watching them now. This was the nightmare she'd been trying to avoid. She tried dancing around the truth, knowing before the words were out of her mouth that it wasn't going to work.

"He isn't—in fact, he has a nice town house on—"

"But he *was*, wasn't he, Pam?" Martin sneered.

"That's enough—enough already," Ted stepped in. "What's wrong with you people? I lived at the shelter, yes. I got myself together at a point where I needed some help. Maybe you all have had it easy, but it's not like that for everyone. I have a job, and a home, and a wonderful woman to share my life with. Besides that, I don't see how this is anyone's damned business but our own. Pam's done nothing she needs to explain to any of you, and neither have I."

Pam looked up at Ted, shaking her head, the

questions in her mind bursting out before she could stop them.

"Why? Why would you say all that?"

Ted jerked back as if she'd slapped him. She wanted to take back the words—or maybe not. The public declaration left her no wiggle room, no place to hide. Everyone knew now, and while that might be fine and dandy for Ted, the lives of twelve other people who hadn't quite gotten their feet under them still depended on her.

Now that the cat was out of the bag, she knew they'd be losing donor support left and right. How would she manage to keep the shelter open? What would happen to those people who lived there? This was terrible.

"I'm sorry," Ted offered in an overly controlled tone of voice that didn't quite mask his hurt. "I said it because it's true. Why should they be attacking you because you didn't want to date *this* guy?" He glared at Martin again. "We're consenting adults— we don't owe anyone explanations."

She nodded, not knowing what else to do, unable to say a word. Mr. Douglas solved that problem again.

"Well, while that may be the case, and you certainly are free to date whomever you wish, you can forget what we talked about earlier, Ms. Reynolds. I had questions about supporting your organization as it was. Considering this new development, I know that I for one do not want to be associated with such a scandalous arrangement."

"Mr. Douglas, you don't understand—"

"I understand very clearly."

With that, he turned and left. People started clearing away from their table, murmuring and whispering, leaving only Ted and Pam looking at each other hopelessly.

"What now?" Ted asked miserably.

Pam shook her head. "I don't know, Ted. I just don't know."

JOY DIDN'T WORRY ABOUT her dreams that night because she didn't fall asleep. Even though she'd assured Rafe that she didn't want to engage in any more sensual explorations that evening, they'd shared a glass of wine, a tentative kiss good night, and he'd left.

She wanted to be relieved, but she wasn't. All she could think about was how his erection had weighed in her palm, how thick and hard he'd been, and how his desire had touched her at depths of need she hadn't known she had.

She could recall the nuance of every moment, how he'd kissed her, the sounds he'd made, as if he was really enjoying himself, really turned on by her—and the end result seemed to imply that was the case. Still, that wasn't so unusual for guys, right? It was easier for them.

It was much more difficult for her to think about giving herself over that way. The incident by the door was easy—it was all about him. Though she couldn't fault him for offering to do his part—truth was, she was scared.

She was also excited.

She was a mess, actually.

Though she'd sent him home tonight, she'd agreed to *fun*. She was hoping maybe she really could reach down and find the key to loosening up with a guy like Rafe. Could she enjoy being with a man who appealed to her, and her alone? Someone who tempted her to take a chance? She blocked the recurring thought that her father would give her "that look" if he knew she was carrying on with an unemployed ambulance driver.

Her father wasn't here, and she was an adult woman, making her own choices. Pam was right— Joy needed to take control and stop worrying so much about what her father would approve of or not, or if her dates met some weird, invisible standard of perfection. That way of thinking hadn't exactly led to a stellar love life so far.

Tossing to the other side of her bed, she threw the blanket off, sweating, though cool night air was drifting in from the screen. She hesitated, wondering if Rafe was watching her. The erotic possibility had her squeezing her legs together, trying to quell the need that pulsed through her.

Was he over there, as hot as she was? Lying awake, wondering about her? Wishing he was here with her? Or did the satisfaction she'd helped him find earlier lead him to the night's rest he so ardently desired? Selfishly, she hoped he was wide awake.

She sank her teeth into her lip. *Fun.* It might be fun to pull the curtain to the side and switch the low light of her closet on, illuminating the room slightly, enough so he could see. Could she do it?

Do you ever have any fun?

Rafe's question taunted her in the darkness, and she thought maybe she could have some fun right now. She could tempt him from the window. If he was watching, maybe he'd come back over and help her ease the ache that was keeping her awake, and they could have some fun together.

Her heart beat erratically in anticipation, and she turned the light on low, knowing no one else could see down the side of the house unless they were right outside. Or in Rafe's house. It would be a private show.

Slipping her nightgown from her body, she crawled back onto the bed, lying back and drumming up the courage for what came next, when she heard a knock at the door.

"Wow, that was fast," she commented with a grin, launching herself out of bed and grabbing her robe on the way downstairs. As she belted it, she wondered if maybe she should abandon it and answer the door naked—that would be fun, right?

It would also mean standing in her doorway with nothing on—while it was the middle of the night, you never knew who might be walking down the street. It was enough that she was naked underneath.

Her hands trembled slightly as she turned the burnished brass knob, feeling like the naughtiest girl alive for beckoning a man from her window. Swinging open the door with a smile, she stepped back, her mind blank with surprise when she didn't find Rafe, ready and willing, but Pam, sobbing and miserable.

"Pam! What happened? Come in. Oh, my god, honey, what's wrong?"

Pam's makeup was streaked and her hair was disheveled, as if she'd run her hands though it repeatedly.

"I broke my shoe on your stair," she said between sobs, and somehow Joy knew that wasn't the source of her friend's unhappiness.

"Come here, sit down. I'm sorry about your shoe, but what happened?"

Joy grabbed a box of tissues on the entry table and handed them to her.

Pam blew her nose noisily and took a few gulping breaths, then managed to croak out a few clear phrases, not looking or sounding like the canny, self-assured woman Joy had always known.

"Oh, Joy." She took another deep breath, her body shaking with the effort to control her sobs. "I don't know what's going to happen now...."

"Listen, how about a glass of wine and we can talk?"

"I—I'm s-so sorry, to w-wake you up...."

"You didn't—I was awake anyway, and you probably saved me from making an ass of myself."

Pam looked at her curiously through bloodshot, tear-filled eyes, and Joy shook her head. "Not worth discussing—let me get the wine, and don't worry, you're sleeping here tonight."

Joy knew her friend's sudden appearance had saved her from making a colossal error in judgment. She didn't like seeing Pam so upset, but she'd almost made a huge mistake.

She'd told Rafe that she wanted to take things slowly and see what happened. Five hours after saying that, she'd been ready to do a naked peep show for him from her bedroom window. Her wants, needs and desires were seriously confused, and rushing matters wasn't going to help any.

She poured two glasses of wine, emptying the bottle that she and Rafe had opened for dinner, and handed one to Pam.

"Okay. Now, what happened?"

Joy could swear she'd never seen anyone in this much emotional pain since her mother had walked out the door on her father. Pam was usually so stalwart and strong, not letting much get to her, and Joy had always admired that. Right now, though, her friend looked completely done in.

"Oh, God, Joy. Everything is such a wreck. It was all so perfect twelve hours ago. Well, not perfect, but perfect enough, you know? If only I hadn't gone to that stupid party…"

Joy leaned in, trying to make sense of the stream of comments.

"Something bad occurred at the party?"

"It was a disaster—well, at first it was wonderful to be out with Ted, dancing, and the place looked beautiful, with all the lights and the tree…." Pam stopped, gulping to control breaking into sobs again.

Joy grabbed more tissues. "Here. Cry away, then talk."

Through her sobs, Pam managed to tell Joy, in detail excruciating enough that Joy completely shared her friend's embarrassment and pain.

"That Solese! He's such a pig—he came on to me, too, back then!"

Pam's astonishment stemmed her tears. "Are you kidding?"

"Nope. He caught me in the kitchen at the shelter one day, I was packing some lunches, and he got in my personal space a little too much. When I asked him to back off, he asked me out. I turned him down flat, of course. He didn't like the rejection—I think he might have gotten mad at me, but one of the residents came in, and he left."

"Why didn't you ever tell me?"

"I never thought about it again, to be honest. He was so annoying."

Pam nodded. "Well, his annoyance translated into a big scene tonight, and that scene might make some serious trouble for me—we could be shut down by the end of January if people stop their donations. If the papers get hold of this, maybe faster."

Joy threw her hands up. "I don't get it—it's not like you house teenagers or vulnerable populations. These are grown men. Ted's an adult, and you have an adult relationship. How is he doing in all of this?"

Joy knew she'd hit the big nerve when she saw fat tears rolling down Pam's cheeks.

"H-he… We're not together anymore." The last word was choked out on another sob.

"What do you mean you're not together? How can that be?"

"We were so angry with each other, I guess. We left, and drove down to the Seaport and walked, and he was in his 'too bad about them, what do we care?' mode, and I had to remind him that twelve other lives are depending on me and keeping that shelter open right now. His open declaration threatened that—who knows how bad it will be if word gets around?"

Joy sat back, pensive. Pam was in a terrible spot,

and she didn't know exactly what to say to make her feel better, so she chose her words carefully.

"I can see how you were both pushed into impossible corners. I don't blame him for wanting to come out and say you're together—he's right, why should you be ashamed?" Joy said, holding a hand up to stem Pam's quick response. "I can also see that you're right, too—it's about more than the two of you. You have worked so hard to make Second Chance what it is, and it's directly responsible for how successful Ted has become. He should have realized that."

Pam raised a hand to her face, quieter now, but seeming almost emptied out.

"He does know, which is making him feel guilty for what he did, though he shouldn't—you know? It also means the people at the shelter will probably find out, and that could screw things up there. You know how they see me as a mother, or like a boss, at least. This could diminish me in their eyes."

"Because you fell in love? How can they miss how wonderful this is? They would all be inspired to work for the same in life, I think."

Pam smiled wanly. "That's true, but as you know some of them aren't 'there' yet—they've faced such hard times, and they rely on me as the steady presence, the rock…. If they think I might leave, abandon them, well… Or there could be any number of responses I could imagine, none of them good."

"All the more reason for you and Ted to provide a united front. You should talk to the residents together, explain, and Ted could make sure they understand. I think they'd be happy for you."

Pam shrugged, draining her wine.

"It's all too complicated. That may or may not be the right way to go. I have some people I can ask, counselors at other agencies. They can help. I don't know if Ted and I will be getting back together—he was hurt, I was hurt, a lot of angry things were said."

"Oh, Pam, that happens in the best of relationships. People overcome worse all the time—you know that. What's your motto?"

Pam closed her eyes, shaking her head.

"No, come on. You know every single one of those guys who has come in has lost hope and then they find you. What do you tell them?"

"There's no challenge so huge you can't take it on one step at a time," Pam repeated tiredly, a phrase she'd used a million times with others.

"And?" Joy prompted.

"Okay, okay. Sheesh. And if you argue for your limitations, you get to keep them."

Joy smiled, setting her glass on the table.

"I never knew how annoying those sayings were until now," Pam muttered, and Joy laughed.

"A joke! All is not lost if you can make a joke!" she cheerfully offered one more of the many motivational truisms she'd heard Pam share over the years. Corny as they were, they cut to the truth of things, and they worked.

"This may be more than we can—"

"Stop—no arguing for your limitations, remember?"

Pam sighed heavily, giving in. "Okay. Okay. I'll find out tomorrow how bad it is, and we'll get started trying to save face."

"Maybe it won't be as bad as you think. You could start by adopting some of Ted's attitude— while he made an error in making his announcement when he did, he's right. You don't have to apologize for the fact that you're with him. You shouldn't."

"I know. I'm used to giving everything I have to the shelter. I've done that for years, and I don't know how to separate it all out."

"You could start by calling Ted. You two need to talk more now that you're calm."

Pam nodded, her eyelids drooping.

"Time for sleep. Tomorrow is a new day," Joy quipped and offered Pam a blanket.

"Please, stop. I can't take any more motivation now."

"Okay, see you in the morning."

Pam burrowed down into the large sofa, and Joy milled around for a bit, making sure she had settled down before heading to bed.

Looking out her window, she saw the lights on in Warren's house. Rafe was up at this late hour. Her notion of acting the temptress had her shaking her head as she crawled back into bed. Something was tipping all of their worlds sideways lately. Hell, she'd almost opened the door stark naked to her friend tonight. Poor Pam had saved her from seriously embarrassing herself. She'd have to tell her that when she was feeling better. Maybe.

As Joy lay in bed, she mulled for long minutes on whether she had actually experienced a ping of disappointment when it hadn't been Rafe at the door, but sleep saved her from having to admit it.

9

RAFE HADN'T SLEPT AT ALL, his body and mind wired from the interaction with Joy. He'd meant what he'd said. He wanted to get to know her, to have some fun, to help her loosen up. No pressure. He'd have someone to share the holidays with, and maybe they could exert a little physical energy together. All good things.

Glancing down at the insistent morning stiffy he had thinking about it, he hoped they might be able to do that sooner rather than later. She was as wound up as he was, and ready to explode. The repressed desire inside of her and the hungry desperation of her kiss told him that they could share a very merry Christmas together, indeed.

After making his way to the shower, his eyes tired from the lack of sleep though he wasn't as groggy as usual, he stepped under the hot water and thought about the moment by Joy's door.

He had no doubt they would be good together, in spite of her worries. He soaped himself, wondering who had instilled such doubt in her mind about her own sexuality, and why it had taken such deep root. Whoever it was, the guy must have been a bastard. Joy kissed like an angel, he thought, remembering how soft her mouth had been, arousal shooting through him. Rinsing off, his palm curled around his cock, which was demanding attention.

As tempting as it might be, he resisted, backing off. Taking off a little steam never bothered him, but in this case, he wanted to wait—he wanted to stay in this suspended state of arousal, looking forward to what it would be like when he finally could show Joy how much fun they could have together.

His fingers moved instead to the shower dial, switching the water from hot to cold, solving the problem the old-fashioned way. Within moments he was back out, drying off and reaching for his jeans with a keen sense of expectation about seeing Joy later that day. Tonight would have to be soon enough, and in the meanwhile, he had enough house projects to keep him busy and pass the day.

As he was about to leave the house, however, Joy pulled into her driveway. He stopped and got out of the car, crossing the lawn to meet her.

"Hey—what are you doing home?"

She looked tired, as if she'd been up all night, as well. "I was going to go in late, but Ken actually told me to take a personal day—we had a great day yesterday, and he's in a generous mood, so I took him up on it. Pam came by in the middle of the night with a problem, and I'm exhausted after staying up with her."

"Who's Pam?"

"Oh. A good friend. She runs the organization where I volunteer."

"Is she still here?"

"No. She left before I got up, but I thought I'd justify my day off by making some cookies for the shelter, so I went to get some supplies."

"That's nice. Want help?"

She'd been talking to him over her shoulder as she was taking grocery out of the car, and finally she turned, their eyes meeting in a flash of heat.

"Um, sure," she said, smiling. He nearly cheered out loud. Progress. "I haven't baked anything for a while, so I can't guarantee how successful this will be—do you know how to make cookies?"

"I know how to eat them," he joked, taking two of the bags and walking with her toward the house.

"You can be the taste tester then. That way we'll know that no one at the shelter will die from eating my cookies."

"Oh, thanks, that's just swell," he responded with mock sarcasm, chuckling as they went inside. "So," he said, following her into the kitchen and noticing the blankets still thrown over the living-room sofa where her friend must have stayed. "What kind of crisis did your friend have?"

"Oh, it's with her love life, but unfortunately it could also mean trouble for Second Chance."

He frowned as her voice broke on the last, and he realized she'd stopped unpacking things from the bags.

"You okay?"

She shook her head. "Sorry. I'm worried about the shelter. Pam has some potentially serious trouble, and I want to help. Maybe I could pass some thoughts by you, get your take?"

Rafe was surprised, and flattered. "Sure. Go ahead."

"I want to find a way to offset the rumors circulating about the place—undeservedly—maybe some sort of event to show people how much good Pam does for the local community."

Rafe took over unpacking the groceries, leaving items on the counter and said, "Why don't you tell me what the problem is?"

Joy related most of Pam's dilemma as succinctly as she could. To her relief, Rafe didn't particularly see the issue with two consenting adults getting together, regardless of their backgrounds. However, he also knew the world could be far more judgmental, and said só. She warmed to him even more for being so accepting.

"I'll give you what feedback I can, but it sounds like you're already on the right track."

He held out his hand. She took it, and there was

a spark of something in her eyes that he liked very much.

No one was more surprised than he was when she launched herself forward into his arms. He was taken off guard, but not about to argue. Joy had a lot of emotion riding under the surface, and he wondered what it would be like when she really let go.

"Hey, I like this," he teased.

She drew back, looking at him seriously, the way she always did, but her eyes were brighter.

"Thanks, Rafe. It's nice to have someone to spend the day with, making cookies, bouncing ideas around. I'm so used to being by myself, but I like your company. A lot. The whole thing with Pam, with this guy she likes, well, it has me wondering how much we miss if we worry too much about what other people think."

"That's a good point. You have to make decisions that are right for you," he said in a low tone, his eyes dropping to her mouth.

He knew what a huge step it was for her to be open with him, to share her thoughts and ask his opinion, and the urge to kiss her was killing him. When she didn't move away, he gave in, dipping forward to taste her lightly, then more deeply until they were winding around each other, breathless. He walked her backward a few steps until she bumped into a chair and lost her footing. Steadying themselves, she laughed and pushed the hair back from her flushed cheeks.

"Maybe we should make those cookies."

He nodded, his heart pounding from the kiss, his erection straining against his jeans. He could think of better ways to spend the day, but that wasn't what Joy needed right now.

"Tell me what you want me to do, and I'm yours," he said, knowing she'd pick up on the not-so-subtle innuendo in his offer. He meant every word.

BY FOUR O'CLOCK, the house was hot from the oven, as well as the sun shining in all day. Cookies surrounded her and Rafe on every side—all surfaces of the kitchen were covered with cooling, decorated or soon-to-be-decorated cookies.

Baking hadn't been that difficult, really, and it had been fun. They'd worked together easily while brainstorming ideas to help the shelter. Rafe actually was a wonderful sounding board, and he was very creative, and told her what he thought honestly. She was even more excited about her ideas now and couldn't wait to tell Pam. She felt so good to be doing something, not sitting around worrying.

Joy peeked at Rafe while he stood sprinkling sugar in a very precise, male fashion over a tray of frosted goodies—he was gorgeous, inside and out. He was so easygoing, happy to help. He genuinely seemed to like her company, too. Warmth stole through her, and she bit her lip, watching him. The T-shirt he wore was a little damp from the heat and stuck to his skin, revealing the strong muscles of his back, and she lowered her gaze to other delectable regions.

Rafe might be surrounded by sweets, but he was a sexy confection all by himself. She chuckled out loud, and covered her hand to her lips a moment too late. He turned, looking at her, a dab of green sugar at the corner of his lips.

"What's so funny?" he asked, unaware.

"You've been sampling again," she accused, her eyes transfixed on the sugar.

Following the direction of her stare, he started to lift his hand to remove the evidence, but she stepped forward, halting him. She shut off her mind and followed her instincts for once. It was about time she started taking some of the opportunities for fun that came her way.

"Let me," she offered, her heart beating furiously as she slipped a hand behind his neck and lifted up to dart her tongue out and lick the sugar away.

He lasted for two strokes of her tongue against his skin until he pulled her up close with a groan and took over, backing her into the counter and kissing her so hard and so thoroughly that she couldn't breathe, but air was highly overrated anyway. If she'd thought the temperature was hot in the kitchen before, it was rising by degrees as he kissed her.

"Joy, I want you something fierce," he murmured

in her ear, pressing the promise of his erection against her hip. Tension twisted inside of her, invading the moment—should she?

His hand slipped under the T-shirt she was wearing, finding her breasts, closing and rubbing, plucking and caressing the sensitive tips into hard points against his palm. Oh, my, he knew what he was doing, and her body responded to his dedicated, confident touch.

"You like that? How about this?"

Pulling her shirt off right there in her kitchen, he had her topless before she could object, not that she planned to. It was scandalous—the windows were open; she could hear voices out in the yard where a woman next door visited someone else across the fence. They couldn't see…but they were there, and she and Rafe were…*ohhh.*

He suckled her so sweetly she dug her fingers into his hair and she managed to quell her moan to a whimper, lest she be heard through the screen door. When he drew away, lapping her skin with his tongue, she objected with a muted groan.

"Come here," he said, his eyes wicked as he grasped a bowl of frosting they'd been using for cookies.

She held perfectly still, unbearably aroused as he used the soft spatula to completely frost her breasts. Her skin was so hot she figured the confection would melt right off her skin. Rafe smiled devilishly, reaching for some red cinnamon sprinkles. Her eyes went wide.

"Rafe, what are you doing?"

"Decorating you—you are plenty tasty enough all on your own, but this is fun—isn't it?" He looked at her intently, and she had no choice but to agree.

"Yes, it is."

He took great care in "decorating" her, and she thought she would go crazy, dying for his mouth on her, waiting interminable minutes before he stepped back to admire his masterpiece. He yanked off his own shirt and hauled her against him for a deep kiss.

"You ruined all that hard work," she whispered breathlessly as he released her, icing and cinnamon candies smeared all over his chest now, as well.

"Now we get to share," he said with an evil wiggle of his eyebrows, making her laugh, then moan, as he began licking away the frosting with dedicated thoroughness, his tongue washing every inch of her clean, her body on fire and writhing as he did. She was short of begging him to take her by the time he finished, and she knew he could tell that when he looked at her.

"Do you want this, Joy? Do you want me?"

She'd never wanted anything more. He was like every dream she'd ever had—literally—coming true. But even her dreams, while hot, hadn't been this fun, this real.

She held his gaze, nodded, and he smiled in

heartfelt relief, as if he'd been poised on an edge, waiting. The fact that he seemed to have held his breath for her answer made her feel special. Within seconds he was naked and so was she. A tray of cookies slid noisily to the floor as he made room for her on the counter, his movements sure but urgent.

She couldn't believe a man, let alone a man like Rafe, wanted her this badly. She could see in the way his eyes raked over her, in the hardness of his body and the tremble of his hand, how much he needed her.

"I've never done this before…on a kitchen counter, I mean," she said hesitantly, watching him grab a condom from his wallet and slide it over his shaft. She was on the pill, but didn't protest. The next thing she knew, he was flush up against her, that delicious part of him sliding against her heat, though he didn't make his way inside.

"I hope you'll find this worth sacrificing a few cookies for," he teased, planting his palm on the crease of her hip and thigh, his thumb rubbing the hot slit of her flesh, making her gasp in delight. His hand was large and warm, his fingertips slightly rough, probably from the work he was doing on Warren's house, and the sensations his touch brought forth were mind-blowing.

"What cookies?" she joked breathlessly, arching against him. She curled her fingers around the counter's edge, positioning herself and opening for him as he eased inside of her, big and hot, filling her completely. She trembled with the completeness of it. Yes, this was better than her dreams—and her dreams had been pretty damned good.

"Definitely worth trashing the cookies," she said, hearing him chuckle as he began to move, rocking his hips in a steady rhythm, finding her mouth with his and parrying his tongue with hers in the same way.

There was a delectable pressure building in-side—something she couldn't remember experiencing with another man, ever.

Rafe couldn't seem to stop kissing her, her mouth, her face, her neck, murmuring hot words now and then, but mostly his lips were engaged in kissing every spot of her he could reach as he drove himself forward with increasing speed, touching her everywhere, urging her to come along with him.

She wanted to—she honestly did. Satisfaction hovered on the edge like a lightning bolt on the horizon, ready to strike, but the moment she became conscious of it, the brightness disappeared.

She groaned in frustration—why, *why* couldn't she do this simple thing? Her body was obviously willing, though her mind wouldn't let go. Sex was in the brain, so they said, and she seemed like living proof. Her brain was completely out of sync with her body.

Knowing it wasn't going to happen, she didn't intend to risk Rafe's disappointment. They'd had a perfect day, and she wasn't going to let on that she couldn't live up to his expectations.

Turning her attention back to the moment, she relished the strong grip of his hands on her backside, how his fingers pressed in as he buried his face in her neck. Following his gentle cues, she lifted her legs up over his shoulders, increasing the intensity of the vocals she made, indicating she was reaching her climax, and loving how he responded by hammering even harder into her, throwing his head back. She watched him, not entirely minding that she wasn't completely in the moment; it was worth it just to observe the wild intensity with which he made love to her.

She'd never seen a man so utterly open and un-inhibited—and with *her.* The idea that he reacted to her this way touched a chord deep inside. She couldn't stop watching him.

No sooner had she become aware of the glimmer of possibility than his jaw clenched tight until he let out a grown of release, fitting himself so tightly into her that she was sure even air couldn't move between them as he finished. He pulled her against him, his chest heaving breaths of spent passion.

Her body slid against his, both of them sweaty and slick as he lifted her back down to the floor. She cuddled against him, enjoying the moment. He felt so good to her, there was no denying that.

As their breathing settled, he rubbed her back

and stepped away a little, looking down into her face. He looked more relaxed, more handsome, if that was even possible.

"That was wonderful," he said, and she nodded, not quite meeting his gaze, kissing his shoulder.

"Yes, it was."

He backed up another step, framing her face in his palms and looking at her with a gaze so penetrating she nearly had to turn away. "Joy, I know a lot about the human body, and about women. What I don't know is why you'd fake it with me."

"What do you mean?"

"Joy," he said in gentle admonition, and she moved away, bending to reach for her clothes.

"Fine, I faked. So what? It was nice anyway, I enjoyed it—I think I might have come close, but I typically don't…I've rarely been able to, uh…"

"Orgasm," he stated bluntly.

She looked away stubbornly, pulling on her underwear and her shirt. "Yes."

"Why didn't you tell me instead of pretending?"

"I didn't want to make it bad for you—I didn't want you to be disappointed."

"Why would I be disappointed? How could it be bad? It was incredible. A lot of women have trouble in that department, and if you'd told me, I could have done something else."

His voice lowered to a sexy pitch when he said the simple words *something else,* making her flutter all over in response, but she also didn't know what to say. No man had ever talked to her this bluntly before—none had cared, happy to enjoy themselves and go on their way. She'd gotten used to it, and Rafe's penetrating gaze and questions made her squirm, awkward and exposed.

He put his hands on her arms, making her face him.

"Listen, okay, fine," she said blusteringly. "I know this is a guy thing, you like to know you can make us respond, and I did respond, Rafe, as best I could. I loved what you did, but I'm too uptight. I think too much, and I can't turn it off. It's not you, it's me," she joked lamely.

Joy felt on edge, probably because her body was still riled up. Rafe didn't make it easy; he didn't let her off the hook, and she didn't know exactly how to deal with it. Rafe didn't want spin, he only wanted the truth.

"Joy, we can try lots of different things, whatever you want," he said quietly. Leaning in to kiss her, she didn't kiss him back, but didn't draw away, either. "Let me show you—we can experiment, play, whatever."

Joy wanted to believe that, but she knew…she just *knew* that as long as her mind was engaged, she wasn't going to be able to loosen up enough to find satisfaction. The wheels in her mind spun around an idea, one she wasn't sure she should speak out loud. Would he think she was a total freak?

Regardless of her doubts, she wanted badly to be

with Rafe—she wanted so much to believe what he was saying, and there might be one way they could both enjoy their time together.

"You're open to anything?"

"As long as it doesn't involve serious physical injury, animals or shaving off my body hair, yes. Anything."

She laughed. He made her laugh so easily. That was a good thing, wasn't it?

"My doctor told me my little problem wasn't anything physical—I'm mentally blocked. I can, uh, you know…help myself," she admitted, and saw his eyes blaze with interest. "Then there are my dreams…. Nothing holds me back in dreams, so it's only a problem when I'm awake, apparently," she tried to joke, but it fell flat.

"That's good to know," he said, not laughing, either, touching her face gently.

"So I'm thinking, maybe we should try being together at night. You know, if you come over and sleep here, and I start to dream…I think I would be less…repressed, just then."

His brow furrowed, and she held her breath, afraid he would refuse.

"I'm all for spending the night in your bed, Joy—but are you saying you want me to have sex with you while you're sleeping?"

She fidgeted, but decided to boldly state her case, since he had said he'd do *anything*.

"Well, I mean, I have these hot dreams, and they're about you anyway, and maybe if you're there, then if things start up, and maybe my mind would be as receptive as my body. I do want you, Rafe."

He pulled on his jeans, taking a moment to think.

"I see your point, but I wouldn't want to startle you, or worse, while you're sleeping. Chances are those dreams are about more than sex. Maybe if we spend some time during the day together, and get to know each other a little, that would help, too. You know, the Japanese sometimes make foreplay last all day long, or longer, before actually having sex." He smiled naughtily. "I think we've gotten a good start in that area."

"Oh," was all she could say. The thought of all-day foreplay with Rafe made her knees weak.

"So why don't we clean this mess up and take a shower—" he looked down at the frosting dried to his chest "—and then we can head down to the shelter to talk with your friend."

"You want to come to the shelter?"

"Sure, I want to help if I can."

Joy chewed on her lip, thinking. "I don't know. It's probably not anything you really want to bother with, seeing as you're just here for—"

"Joy," he said, cutting her off.

"Huh?"

"Don't close me out, and don't make what's between us low—I'm not just here for sex."

She cleared her throat. "I was going to say, as you're just here for a few weeks."

"Oh. Whoops." He slanted an embarrassed grin, but recovered quickly. "Well, I want to help, if I can. It's less than a week before Christmas, and you have an ambitious plan, so I'll be another set of hands. I'd like to be part of this with you, even if for a little while."

She didn't know why having him come to the shelter was so difficult, as if she were sharing more with him now than her body. Still, his appeal was sincere. He'd listened to her all day and had some good ideas.

"Okay. I appreciate that."

"Thanks. It'll be a fun day. And then..." His voice trailed off, but he was smiling in a way that made her blood warm and her muscles loose.

"And then?"

"I want to spend the night with you, Joy—I'd like to spend every night that I'm here with you. I've got enough of an ego that I'd like you to be awake when I'm inside of you. I want you to know you're with me, not just in your dreams, flattering as that is. I want you to know it, remember everything I do to you."

The way he said it made her melt. She remembered quite well what it was like when he filled her body with his own, and she would like to be awake for that, too.

"I know. Me, too. Maybe this is a way to get to that point?"

He pulled her close. "Sure…but first let's go take that shower."

10

JOY SAT IN THE MEETING, trying to concentrate, but her focus was not on the job at hand. She made eye contact with Ken, nodded, scribbled down a note, and then her thoughts wandered off. She couldn't wait for this endless meeting to cease. Who really cared about what colors of certain toys sold better than others? Did she?

Not really.

However, she did care about being able to pay her mortgage, so she made another effort, listening intently to what was being said, only to find her mind drifting off yet again.

The routine tasks in her work bored her to death, if she were to be completely honest. She had more important things to think about, like the fund-raising event at Second Chance. Pam had loved the idea, but they were all busting their backsides to make it work—it was five days to Christmas and counting.

Christmas had suddenly taken over her life. Rafe was decorating everything in sight—including her, she thought naughtily, knowing she'd never think about frosting the same way again.

Along with Pam, they were throwing a Christmas bash at the shelter for the community at large, as well as businesses and organizations they wanted to reconnect with. It was a more personal way to put a kibosh on the rumors that might be spreading about Pam and to show how much good the place did in the community. Joy knew people would be impressed if they came and saw the place, met Pam and met the people who lived there.

She had so much to do to get ready. She also had to polish her final presentation for her official interview with the board for the promotion, and yet she found herself curiously less excited about that prospect. With Rafe, the holidays, Second Chance… there was so much going on, she was losing track of her priorities, she thought. Or they were shifting, which was a much more disconcerting prospect. She'd always known what she wanted, hadn't she? Rafe was showing her a whole other side to herself that made her think maybe she should want more.

Between the sheets of paper that comprised her notes, she sneaked out her list of people to contact, reviewing it, strategizing the best way to approach each one. She planned to purchase formal invitations—bought with her own money—to send in the mail as well. She didn't plan on accepting a refusal from anyone, if it meant she had to drive them to the party herself.

For the first time in as long as she could remember, she had an attitude resembling Christmas spirit. A sense of anticipation was in the air, though she knew that was mostly due to the prospect of seeing Rafe soon. They'd spent a cuddly night together the evening before, and she'd slept better than ever, wrapped up in Rafe's arms as he stroked her back. No dreams had come to her—she'd been so exhausted that she had been too tired to dream. Unfortunately, she'd apparently been too tired for anything else, as well.

When she'd awakened, Rafe had been propped up in bed, fully clothed, reading. He'd had shadows under his eyes, and she knew he hadn't slept. For the first time, she'd realized the extent of his problem—people talked about losing sleep, having insomnia, but she realized that Rafe really was awake, all day and then all night, unable to sleep. She couldn't imagine it. How did he maintain any energy at all? Yet he'd gotten out of bed and had gone for a run as she'd left for work. Astonishing.

He'd left her with a kiss so hot she could still taste him; she closed her eyes and relived the moment. She wanted to rock his world, to ride him into exhaustion and give him the best night's sleep of his life—it had become a personal goal.

She grinned secretly as she played out the

naughty fantasy in her mind, imagining what it might take to exhaust Rafe. When a vibration buzzed softly in the pocket of her suit jacket, she jumped, emitting a little squeak of surprise, her face flooding with heat as everyone turned to look at her.

She plucked the cell phone out, smiling in apology and peeking at the most recent hot text message from Rafe. He'd been sending them all morning, part of his "all-day foreplay" plan. It certainly had spiced up her day, that was for sure.

Reading the current message, she wiggled a little in her chair, completely blanking out on the fact that she was being addressed.

"Joy? Are you with us?"

She blinked, setting the cell phone down on the table. Then realizing the people next to her might see the text message, she quickly snatched it up, fumbling it in her fingers, nearly sending it spinning across the table. Holding her breath, she managed to finally stick the phone back into her jacket pocket as it started vibrating again.

When she looked up, she saw that Ken was watching her impatiently.

She hadn't been caught in a situation like this since she'd been bold enough to pass notes in fifth grade and had had hers read aloud to the class. She wondered if Ken would have read her text message aloud if he'd grabbed her phone, and her naughty smile twitched again.

"I'm sorry, what?"

Ken cleared his throat. "I know it's the holiday and everyone is distracted, but I asked if you had worked out the media campaign for the Pearson project?"

"Oh, yes, of course," she said, pulling herself together and distributing her copies around the room, then quickly starting to review the main points, when Ken interrupted her.

"Joy," he started, and she looked up quickly.

"Yes?"

"What is this? This isn't the right paperwork."

She glanced down and realized that she'd made copies of the party-planning list for the shelter, not her media plan.

"Oh, I'm sorry—this is for another project…." she apologized, her naughty humor disappearing as she gathered the papers. "I can go over the budget verbally, I know it like the back of my hand, I'm so sorry for this, there's a lot going on this time of year you know—"

"What project is this? I didn't know we were planning a Christmas event," he inquired.

"It's pro bono work for a homeless shelter on the north side."

Ken looked completely baffled. "Pro bono? What do you mean pro bono? We don't do pro bono."

"It's a personal project."

"How much time have you been putting into it?"

"It's on my own time—I'm running event organization for them. It hasn't cost you anything," she reassured, trying not to sound too biting.

"Apparently, it costs us your focus on our work, and the projects we've put in your lap, I'd say," Ken offered, and she sighed, having no real answer to that.

"You're right. Sorry." Yet was she? She didn't feel sorry. She felt annoyed. She irrationally wanted to tell Ken to cram it, but she knew he was right.

"Well, mistakes happen. You can tell us the high points of the media plan, and we'll want copies directly after the meeting."

She didn't know how she managed to do it, but she did, and when the meeting was over, she couldn't have been more relieved. Ken didn't leave the room, however, but went over to the door, closing it before she had a chance to escape. *Shit.*

"Ken, really, I'm sorry but—"

"Joy, you're one of our best. Maybe the best among your peers at the moment."

She hadn't seen *that* coming and blinked. "Um, thanks."

"I mean it. You're a strong contender for the new position, certainly the most qualified, but the question I need to ask you, is this the best job for you?"

"What?"

"There's no debating you're good at this work, Joy, but do you really want to do it for the rest of your life? The new position will take up even more of your time and energy, and while I don't doubt that you have the mind and the talent for it, I do wonder if you have passion."

"Passion?"

"Yes. You're good at what you do, but I don't often see you excited about it. Lately, that's even more evident. I've worked with you for a while now, and you're competent, efficient, but…it's like you're still holding something back. Honestly, if I had to choose, I'd go with someone who had more passion and fewer qualifications, because passion is what takes you the distance."

She tensed at the criticism. "I didn't know *passion* was a requirement."

"It's not, but it's something we all think about when we're hiring someone to join the executive staff. A passion for the job, the company, the product. A personal connection. If you want this job, Joy, before we make a final decision, I need to know you really want it, and for more than the bigger paycheck. If this is what you want to do day in and day out for years to come. If you have—"

"Passion," she finished for him, flatly.

"Yes. Exactly."

Joy withered, sinking back into her chair, thanking Ken as he left. What could she do? It seemed passion was the thing lacking in her life overall, and she had no idea if she'd ever had it, or how to find it.

RAFE WAS GRINNING ear-to-ear as he pulled into Warren's driveway. He stepped out of the car to see Bessie getting out of her own car across the street, starting to take out sacks of groceries from the trunk. Rafe trotted over to give her a hand. He liked Bessie, and she always fed him when he came over—it reminded him of his own neighborhood back home, where someone was always trying to feed him something. Thankfully his job and time at the gym worked it off.

"Hey, let me give you a hand with those," he said, lifting the bags out of her arms.

"Well, now, they don't make many like you anymore, Rafe. I hope that young woman across the street knows she's found herself a real gentleman," Bessie complimented him. He acknowledged the words with silence, secretly thinking that if this nice old lady knew what plans he had for Joy later that night, she might not think he was much of a gentleman.

"Lots of groceries here," he commented, changing the subject as they walked up the steps. "Doing a lot of cooking this week?"

"Oh yes. Baking for church and for friends—among which you may count yourself—and of course my family will be here soon, so I need to start now. They all have good appetites, and I like to make everyone's favorites," she declared.

Rafe felt a little twinge of loneliness for his own

family. His mother did the same. His favorite was the manicotti that was standard Christmas-Eve fare, along with the homemade custard-and-cheese cannoli. His mouth watered thinking about it.

"You can put those down on the table, thank you very much. Can I make you some lunch?"

He smiled and then shook his head. "Don't tell my mother if you ever meet her, but your soup is as good as hers, Bessie. There isn't much that would keep me from it, but I have a Christmas tree tied to the top of Warren's car, and I need to get it down and inside the house to surprise Joy."

Bessie's eyes sparkled. "Oh, you're a romantic one, too. I'll send some soup over later—enough for both of you."

"We won't say no," he assured her with a wink.

He returned back to his car, and before long had hauled the Christmas tree into Joy's house, along with a boatload of decorations he'd bought at the store. He wasn't going to decorate it for her, but they'd have some fun—and some *fun*—doing it together.

Still, he looked at his watch and wondered where she was. Time had slid by while he'd put up the tree, and he hadn't realized it was already a half hour later than Joy normally came home from work. He knew this was a busy week. Maybe she'd gotten caught up in something. He was willing to wait.

Still, she hadn't replied to any of his text messages after the first few, and he hoped he hadn't ticked her off again. He sat with an old magazine and the undecorated tree until the sun went down and the Christmas lights were all blinking outside the windows. Finally he gave in to his worry and called Second Chance. No, Joy wasn't there, and Pam hadn't heard from her.

By the time he called her cell and left a message, a little chunk of fear had lodged itself in his gut. He'd seen the results of too many times when someone didn't make it home one night, and it was hard for him not to imagine the worst.

Still, what could he do? He didn't really know Joy all that well, certainly not enough to expect her to check in with him.

Worry turned to annoyance, which transformed into irritation and near anger again as he saw her headlights turn into the driveway, then relief took over. She was fine, just late. Going out on the porch, he met her on the steps.

"Hey, you're home late," he observed, unable to keep the slight accusation out of his tone.

"You were waiting for me?"

Something about that stung; they hadn't had firm plans, but he thought it was pretty clear they were getting together that evening. The fact that she obviously hadn't even given him a second thought put a big dent in the masculine ego.

"Not really, I just stopped by," he lied, his pride digging in.

"Oh, I'm sorry, Rafe. I was out driving."

"Where?"

"Around. I had to think."

Rafe's irritation dissipated as he detected the tone of confusion in her voice, and he went the rest of the way down the steps and took her hands in his.

"Think about what? Us?"

"No... Sort of. Related. I had to think about why I have no passion."

What the hell?

"This sounds like a conversation we need to sit down for. Did you eat?"

She shook her head and they entered the house. Rafe ordered some takeout and then took her coat, leading her over to the sofa to sit with him. Gathering her in his arms, he drew her near and was gratified when she curled in a little.

"You bought a tree."

"I thought we could have some fun decorating it."

"I haven't had a tree in forever. Never as an adult."

"Really? You did say you aren't that into Christmas."

She twisted to face him. "I'm not, and don't you see, that's it."

"What?"

"At Christmas, when everyone is excited, when

there's shopping and gifts and all these celebrations, I don't get into it. I'm left flat."

"Why is that?"

"My father pretty much gave up on Christmas the year my mother took off with her lover. He would buy me a gift each year and leave it on the kitchen table, but we didn't do trees or any of those things. I think it was too painful for him—it all reminded him of her."

Rafe paused, absorbing what she'd said. "She took off at Christmas?"

"Yeah. He—the man she was seeing—was taking her to Paris for the holiday. So she went. We never heard from her again. I don't even know if she's alive, or where she is," she stated matter-of-factly. She didn't really have any emotional trauma over the issue anymore.

"That must have been a huge blow."

"Yes, it was. Dad was never the same. He worked hard, made a decent living and we had a good life, but I guess our life wasn't glamorous enough for her. He worked a lot, long hours—"

"I meant for you, Joy. Sure it was hard on your father, but he was an adult. What about you? To have your mother leave you like that. How old were you?"

She shifted uncomfortably. "Nine."

"Old enough to know what was happening."

"I understood as much as I was able, yes. I heard them arguing the night she left. I took care of him the best I could—we took care of each other, I guess."

"It sounds like it was difficult for both of you, but to never have Christmas again? That's harsh for a kid."

She shook her head. "I didn't want it either. If I had asked, he would have done it, but it reminded me of everything bad, too, so why bother? I guess I still feel that way about the holiday."

She was partly lying. A few years after her mother had gone, she had often wished her dad could celebrate Christmas with her. She would sometimes sit in school and fantasize what gift he would buy her, or how they might decorate the house or send out cards, the way other kids did. Those things had never happened, and she'd loved him enough not to ask for them. She hadn't wanted to cause him more pain. So she'd shut down her own emotions and memories as well, learned to temper her expectations.

"It wasn't right, Joy, and it obviously affected you—question is how long are you going to let your past dictate your present?"

"Rafe, Christmas is one thing, but I'm not passionate about anything! I'm good at my job, but I'm not wild with excitement about it. I was in a meeting today about the best color for new toys and I could not have cared less. I don't have hobbies or boyfriends, and I'm not even that good at sex, because I'm lacking basic passion. That's it. That's the bottom of it."

Rafe was stunned at the tirade, and not entirely sure how to respond.

"You were led to this conclusion because?"

She dropped her head back, groaning. "Ken, my boss, he told me I was a strong contender, maybe the best, for the new position I wanted."

Rafe smiled, unsure how this fit in, but going with it. "That's terrific news!"

"Yes, but he also suggested that while I am very good at my job, I don't have passion for it. Ken says maybe I should rethink if I want the new position, because it demands *passion*."

She made a face when she said the word, crossing her arms tightly in front of her in what Rafe recognized from life with his sisters as a classic female defensive posture. "This is the one thing that I do not have, apparently, across all areas of my life. I'm passionless."

Rafe wasn't sure how to respond, but he took in her deflated, disgruntled posture as she slumped away from him on the sofa, and did the only thing he could do, under the circumstances. He burst out laughing.

He laughed, in fact, so hard that he started to tear up, and could hardly defend himself against the repeated thumps with the bolster pillow that Joy was hitting him with.

"What is so funny, exactly?" she demanded, up on her knees and lording over him with the pillow, her face fierce, which made him laugh all the more—she made quite the picture.

"You—you are. The fact that you think you don't have any passion is one of the most ridiculous things I've ever heard."

"I don't have it, Rafe, I really don't. It all makes sense now—the job, the sex, everything."

"I personally disagree, especially about the sex, but do you think maybe you might have grown up thinking passion was a bad thing? Passion was the reason your mother left your father, and took off to Europe with another man. So it got a pretty bad rap even when you were a kid."

She sat up straight, and he could see the thought take root in her mind.

Joy sat back on the sofa, stunned by the revelation. She was a thirty-year-old woman who'd spent her life, even as a child, holding tightly onto any emotion, not letting anything squeak out, lest it lead her down the same path her mother had gone. She'd been living her life by rote, and she'd never even known it.

"Joy?"

"Oh, God, Rafe…I've been so stupid. I never even realized what's been missing in my life, how afraid I've been of everything that's asked me to make any small emotional investment. It's all been locked up inside, all this time…."

"Coming out in your dreams, though…I guess it was time for you to have this realization. My mother always says things happen when we're ready for them to happen."

"I don't know how I could have lived this way for so long, not really caring about anything, just going through the motions."

"Well, maybe it's not quite that drastic. You cared about your father enough to set your own needs aside, and you care about your friends, like Pam, obviously, and you care about Second Chance—you seem pretty passionate about that to me. You've been really excited about the party, and even about Christmas, the last few days," he offered.

"I do feel differently about my work at the shelter. I never thought about it as work, per se, so I didn't make the connection to how much more involved I am there than at my regular job. I guess that's what Ken means about passion. I had it, have it, I just didn't see it."

"Well, it can go both ways—I loved my job with complete passion, and I think I might have been a little too obsessed with it, to a degree that I burnt out, and now I have nothing else to do. It's not a great feeling."

She lifted her eyes to his, and the zap of heat in her gaze, of understanding, sympathy, and *passion,* had his heart thumping madly.

"I think you were probably astonishing at your job, but maybe when one passion flags, there's a reason, and it's time to find another," she said softly, reaching up to touch his face. Something good—

something very good—was happening between them, and for the moment, Rafe didn't care to talk about work anymore.

"I never knew passion before. Until you," she confessed.

Rafe rubbed his hands lightly up and down her arms. "You're a passionate woman, Joy. I've known it from the moment I…heard you. Definitely when I touched you."

"Rafe," she whispered as he eased back the jacket from her arms and started unbuttoning her shirt, dragging his knuckle along her collarbone.

"You're so soft…. Your skin is like butter, but you're strong, too. It's very sexy," he added, unhooking her bra and working it downward.

"Rafe…how can you be thinking of sex right now? When we're having this serious talk?"

"I think of sex whenever I look at you, think about you, and most definitely when I'm next to you. You're the first woman to turn me on in a long time, Joy—you have no idea. The insomnia, and the stress from the job…I haven't been with anyone in a while. My passions were robbed from me, too, but you've helped bring them back to life."

His hands covered her breasts, massaging gently, and her heartbeat quickened.

She wound her arms around his neck. "Really? You haven't been with anyone since you started losing sleep?"

"Before that, even. I haven't been in the mood. I don't know why. I still can't sleep, but I sure enjoy being awake more than I have for a long time," he said against her skin as he bent to plant kisses across her midriff. "I am most definitely in the mood."

"Rafe, what about the tree?" she asked, relaxing into his touch and encouraging him to continue his exploration.

"Later," he said as he pulled her close in a deep, promising kiss.

11

RAFE HAD THE MOST gorgeous shoulders she'd ever seen. She loved running her hands over them, squeezing them, watching the muscles bunch and relax as she stroked his skin. A physique like his was built from the hard work of carrying stretchers and lugging heavy equipment. He was solid... everywhere. She slid her hand down between his taut thighs and rested it against the ridge in his jeans, sighing. Yep, solid.

"Tempt me all you want, lady, I'm bound and determined to hold out against your feminine wiles," he quipped, tugging the firm tip of one breast between his lips. When he sucked the tender flesh, darting his tongue over her as he did so, the sensations ignited a desire so fierce that she couldn't think clearly.

"I don't think either of us will hold out for long," she panted. Her clothes gone, she could finally glory in the touch of his lips and hands on her skin. He scraped his beard-roughened cheek against the side of her breast, and she loved it. She wound her hand around the back of his neck, urging him on.

She'd never had sex on her living-room floor—or any floor—before. Lame, but true.

"Hey, what about you?" she asked since he hadn't taken off anything but his shirt.

"There's time…. I want to explore you first," he murmured against her skin, and she moaned when he ran his hand up her leg. Suddenly her mind clicked in again, making her feel too exposed, too much at a disadvantage.

"You could undress, too," she suggested, but when he looked up at her, shaking his head, the hot intentions in his gaze shut her up.

"I don't want to be tempted to go too far. You tempt me, Joy, to the edge of reason. Just lay back, relax… Let me enjoy you…and I want you to enjoy me doing it. I want to show you how much passion you really have," he said gently.

"Oh!" she gasped as his mouth traced a path from her navel down to the slick opening between her legs and back again; every muscle in her body clenching in exquisite expectation.

"You fine with that?" he checked. He did it again, and she could only moan out her agreement.

It was so fine that she widened her thighs, inviting him in. The uncomfortable sensation of exposure had passed, replaced with need.

One delicious lick of his tongue on the oversensitized flesh of her sex had her shuddering. She focused on the sensations as he deepened the intimate kiss, stroking his fingers over her skin, urging her along.

She was more than willing to comply, and wiggled a little. She was even so daring as to raise her hands to her breasts, touching herself. He must have noticed and muttered his approval as he brought her closer and closer to the edge. Yet a part of her still held back. Whatever he wanted her to give, she didn't seem to be able to do it. She was having a hell of a lot of fun, but was unable to release the tightly coiled tension.

Then Rafe withdrew his hot touch and began trailing kisses down her thighs, then back up, bringing himself beside her. He gathered her against him, but she pushed back.

"Rafe?"

He put his lips to hers, the taste and scent of her own essence mingled into the kiss, and a wave of excitement washed over her. She clenched her thighs together, hiding her face in his shoulder, unabashed and yet embarrassed by her own raw neediness.

"I—I want more, Rafe," she begged, planting kisses from the column of his neck to his shoulder, pressing herself into him wantonly. He was still erect, still excited; the heat emanating from his skin was more than she thought a human being could generate.

"I know. Me, too. Now isn't the time."

She looked down over her naked, aroused body. "You stopped because I tensed up," she whispered, dismay replacing her arousal.

He got to his feet, putting his hand out to help her up.

"Yes—because I want you to enjoy it. We have plenty of time. That was nice, and we'll pick up where we left off, don't worry," he promised with a wicked smile. Confused, she reached for her clothes.

"Wait. Don't get dressed," he ordered.

"Why not? It's obvious you don't plan on getting *un*dressed," she said grumpily.

"Don't worry, I will…but we're going to have a little fun first—remember, foreplay all day? No need to rush. We can draw it out, see how long we can last."

"Yeah?" she said, annoyed, but halted with her shirt in her hands, not putting it on. "So what did you have in mind?"

"It's almost Christmas. I brought you a Christmas tree. The traditional thing to do is decorate it."

She'd forgotten about the tree. She hadn't had a tree since she was a child; she didn't have any decorations, even.

Then she spotted the bags on the floor.

Rafe went over to them, and she forgot about the tree again, watching the lovely interplay of muscles along his back, butt and legs, as he moved. She was definitely experiencing some passion.

In a flash, he lost his own clothes. "Naked Christmas-tree decorating," he turned to her and said with a sly grin.

"I *don't* think so," she said, grabbing at her shirt again. "There's sap. Those needles are sharp."

"Nope, I thought of that already. This is a Fraser fir, very soft to the touch. We're completely safe. As for sap, well, that shouldn't be a problem if we're careful, but if you get sticky, I'll wash you off," he said flirtatiously, and she rolled her eyes.

He stood assessing the room, a glint of excitement in his eyes, his hands planted on his hips. She was speechless—this was surely the oddest day of her entire life.

"We can close the curtains while we're decorating."

Joy didn't really care about the tree, but she watched his naked form with great interest. He had a beautiful, sculpted backside, and his front, well, she knew how nice *that* was. He was still semihard as he pulled boxes from the bags without an ounce of self-consciousness. To avoid standing there like a moron, she joined him in the task.

He smiled up at her and she was unexpectedly moved.

"That's the spirit," he said agreeably. "I got all types of decorations. I wasn't sure what you'd like."

"Thank you. I'll pay you back," she said, unsure what else to say, but his hands froze over his task.

"That's not the point, Joy," he said quietly, and she knew she'd stuck her foot in it. "It's a gift."

"Oh, I mean, I didn't mean... *Shit,*" she said, dropping to sit on the sofa. Her body was still throbbing from his abridged seduction, and her brain was on overload trying to process the things happening to her. Now here she sat, naked in her living room with Rafe and a Christmas tree. Freakishly, she didn't seem to care as much about her job at the moment. Was she in denial? Shock?

"Joy?"

"Hmm?" She didn't look up.

"Relax. Unpack the decorations, we'll decorate it, and see what happens. Maybe you'll have fun. Stop thinking it to death."

She sighed heavily into her hands. "Okay. Okay, you're right. Old habits are hard to break. None of this is normal to me."

"Maybe that's a good thing, right?"

"I suppose."

She rooted through the bags and pulled out boxes of lights and decorations.

"First, the lights," Rafe declared.

She looked over at the tree. Staring at it, she could almost imagine snow outside. The image evoked memories and emotions she'd thought were gone, and she wrapped her arms around her middle, shivering.

"Are you okay?" Rafe asked.

"Yes, I'm fine…. I forgot how pretty the trees are."

"They are pretty. I can't imagine Christmas without one."

"I used to have some favorite decorations— they're probably still up in the attic at Dad's."

Rafe was gazing at her with such warmth, concern and understanding that she had to glance away as he spoke. It was as if he knew what was going on inside of her clearer than she did, and she didn't know how she felt about that.

"You ever go back?"

"Not for a while. He remarried last year. He's happier than he has been since I can remember. I think Lois has been good for him, and I know she's insisting he celebrate Christmas. I'm glad for him."

"That's good. What about you? Don't you want to be happy, too?"

She didn't say anything, his words landing home. She looked at the tree again, picking up a string of lights.

"I don't know. I figured if I made the right choices, did the right things, worked hard, then I would be happy. It doesn't seem to always end up that way, does it?"

"Maybe they weren't all the right choices."

She blew out a breath. "Could be," she hedged. "I think we'd better get back to decorating this tree."

He smiled, taking the string of lights. "You're the boss."

Somehow, with Rafe, who had blustered into her life, had her decorating trees and walking around her house naked, among other things, she doubted that, but wasn't about to argue.

They worked in concert, placing the lights, then

moved on to the ornaments. Rafe had bought enough for two Christmas trees, and they'd be lucky if this one didn't topple over once they were done. She was enjoying herself more than she'd anticipated.

"Help. I can't quite reach this branch," she said, stretching to hang a heavy Santa ornament on a thick, stubby branch close to the top. Rafe stepped behind her, slipping a hand around her waist and snuggling close as he took the ornament and hung it from the branch she'd been targeting. She almost dropped the damned ornament, raw desire making her knees weak.

He didn't move away when he was done hanging the decoration, but instead wrapped both hands around her front, his hands doing wicked things to her breasts as he kissed the back of her neck. She leaned against him, the hardness of his cock slipping into the pocket of heat between her thighs as she issued an unmistakable invitation for what she wanted him to do, right now, right there, standing by the Christmas tree. He didn't do anything more than continue to kiss and rub, shifting back and forth with a gentle friction that had them both panting with need.

"Rafe," she said breathlessly, reaching up to touch his face, "let's go upstairs. We'll finish the tree later."

He murmured his agreement, then suddenly the doorbell rang, yanking her out of the spell with a groan.

"Ignore it," she said.

"It's the food," he said, pulling on his jeans and grabbing his wallet. "Just take a sec. I'm starving," he added, dragging his eyes down her form as he said it.

They hadn't had dinner, though she wasn't hungry for anything but more of what Rafe was doing to her body. When he went to the door, she made sure she was out of eyesight, and shivered, missing his heat.

After he set the food on the table, he turned her around in his arms and took her mouth in a kiss so carnal her toes curled into the carpet, and she thought hazily that she might never wear clothes around her house again.

His tongue stroked hers repeatedly before sucking her into his mouth, tasting her deeply, touching her as she wanted him to touch her elsewhere. She'd never, ever, in her life been this turned on by a man's touch. She had a hard time coming, yes, but she was damned near the edge from what he was doing to her mouth, and she wanted more, saying as much when he released her from the kiss.

"We will…after the tree is done. Then we can have some dinner and admire it."

"I don't want to wait," she pleaded, her frustration reaching a fevered pitch. He kissed her again, and her body fit itself to his.

"Just a little longer. Don't be so bossy," he teased, kissing her nose before stepping away to reach for the last few ornaments. Joy wanted to scream but helped him nonetheless, placing the last ones much less thoughtfully than she had at first.

She was hot all over and craving whatever relief Rafe could offer. She'd never been this aroused in her entire life, and while it was all good, she was simultaneously afraid of losing the buzz, as if too much teasing would backfire, like overinflating a balloon and having it burst.

One look at Rafe's very aroused body and she knew her fears were probably baseless. This horny phase she was in wasn't likely to pass until she had him—maybe repeatedly.

PAM WOKE UP SUDDENLY, jerking her head from the desk with a cramp in her neck. Papers she'd been working on were plastered to her cheek. She peeled them off, casting a glance at the clock—it was 11:00 p.m. Another night on the cot in the back. She had to finish working on the budget first, though. Maybe if she crunched the numbers again, she'd find a way to squeeze more out of them.

Even with Joy's help, they would barely be able to afford the kind of party they were trying to give, and every cent counted—it was a last-ditch effort at keeping Second Chance open, outside of taking a loan that Pam had no idea how she'd ever pay back. She hadn't told the current residents what was going on, and didn't intend to, not until it was absolutely necessary.

If the worst happened, she'd already been in contact with some other shelters, and she would make sure her people had places to go. The problem was that the other places offered lodging, but they didn't necessarily offer as much support to get people started in new lives, new jobs, with a new sense of self.

Second Chance was about giving people a step up, not just a place to stay. She'd put everything in her life for the last fifteen years into building this place, and her vision had worked. She wasn't going to lose it without a fight.

The determination to fight was good—it was what she needed to keep herself from thinking about how much she missed Ted. They'd talked a few times on the phone, but the conversations had been stilted and touchy. She was hurt, so was he.

They weren't sure how to approach each other anymore, and she hated it—they'd been comfortable around each other since day one, and now it felt as if there were a huge wall between them. All she wanted was his touch, his kiss, and to be able to lean on him right now, but it wasn't possible.

Well, she'd stood on her own before, and she would now. Her thoughts drifted to her parents, and if she were honest, she'd been tempted to ask them to bail her out. They might do it, but then there would be strings, and she couldn't deal with that. They'd never give her the money without conditions, and that was why she'd never asked. They were good people, basically, but they had a different set of values, and they'd always wanted something different for her than what she wanted for herself.

As she turned her bleary eyes back to the pages spread all over the desk, she jumped when there was a soft knock at the office door. She got up—everyone was usually in their room by now, but someone must have noticed her light on.

As she opened the door, her heart plunged. Ted's large form filled the doorway.

"What are you doing here?" was the first thing out of her mouth, and when she saw him flinch, she instantly regretted her harsh welcome.

"I miss you," he said, his tone raw, matching the emotion in his eyes. "I know I screwed up. I want to make it better, I want us to make it better, Pam. Whatever it takes."

She stepped away, hearing what he was saying, but taken aback by the unexpectedness of it. He looked exhausted, haggard, even in his new suit. He must have come directly from the office. Still, she couldn't deny the happiness that surged inside of her. Maybe the wall between them was crumbling somewhat; maybe there was hope.

"I'm sorry, I didn't mean to snap. I'm tired, and I was just startled to see you so late. I've missed you, too," she admitted, closing the door behind him. "I was going over the budgets."

"Are things okay?"

"No," she said honestly, and she hoped without blame. "It's going to be tighter than tight, but we're throwing everything into a Christmas fund-raiser. We're hoping to turn attitudes around, get things back on track. If not, we won't make it long past the new year, unless I take a loan, but I don't know how the hell I would pay it off if I did. Douglas caused some damage, and Martin didn't exactly help—both of them were more than eager to talk to people around them, and of course they made it all sound so…bad."

He met her gaze, his own lighting with determination. "Let me help. I'm doing okay now, I'll get a raise soon—take the loan you were considering. I can shoulder the payments until you get back on your feet."

She shook her head. "No, I can't do that—you just bought the house, the car…. You have enough—"

"Stop," he said firmly.

She looked up and saw the fire in his gaze. Not anger, but something else, something close.

"If I tell you I can handle it, I can handle it, Pam."

Before she knew it, he was across the room, hauling her up against him. She didn't really have time to think. It felt so good; he was so tall and solid against her, she forgot what she was about to say, anyway.

He gazed down into her face, his large, rough hand stroking her cheek, then her hair. Desire for him throbbed straight down to her core. He'd affected her like this ever since the first time he'd touched her, and it had only grown stronger between them.

"You drive me crazy, Pam. I can't stand being away from you," he said, then lowered his lips to hers and took her in such a deep, erotic kiss that her eager responses spiked and she wound her arms around him, giving as good as she got.

Still, as their mouths mated and their bodies sang with the renewed contact, she became distracted by the bitter aftertaste of beer on his kiss, and drew back.

Ted, thinking nothing of the pause in their contact, took the moment to walk away, take off his jacket, his powerful back and arms visible beneath the white dress shirt. She took in his short brown hair, cut in an almost military style. She knew for a fact that the body under the clothes was as strong and virile as his movements suggested.

"Ted, have you been drinking?" she asked tentatively.

He took off his tie, pausing to look at her. "Yeah, I stopped for a beer after work."

"Oh, and you drove here?"

He threw the tie down on the desk.

"Alcohol was never my problem, Pam, as you well know. It was one beer, with dinner, and I sat and thought through what was happening with us. Then I drove over here. Would you like me to sign in? Take a Breathalyzer?"

She'd never been the brunt of his sarcasm, and it stung her. She'd stepped over the line. She'd insulted him, and tried to soften it.

"Stop, I'm sorry, I didn't mean it that way, I want to make sure you're okay is all."

"That's exactly it—you need to stop taking care of me, at least in that way you do with people here who need the guidance and the counseling. I'm your lover, Pam, I'm the man who loves you and wants to be your husband, have a life with you."

The anguish in his eyes tore at her, and she tried to respond, but nothing she could think of sounded right. He went on. "That's all I want you to see when you look at me, but I know there's always some part of you that sees the guy who came in here with nothing—the homeless bum all those people at the party saw, too."

The accusation was like a slap.

"No! How can you say that? I've never, ever thought of you like that. I don't think of anyone here like that, Ted, but especially not you."

He crossed to her again, taking her in his arms and giving her a heady demonstration of his desires—she had no doubt about the emotion that was between them by the time he spoke again.

His face was flushed, his eyes dark with desire, and she melted when his hardness nudged into her stomach. She wanted him so much it almost hurt. It was clear they were in sync on that. There was something about him—something steely that she hadn't really noticed before. Something new. It sent a shiver of excitement down her spine, but it also made her wary.

"If you mean that, then good," he said against her ear. "I want to help you with the problem here, because I know I was part of causing that problem in the first place, shooting my mouth off at that party. I allowed my needs to take precedence over yours, and I want to make up for that. Like any equal partner would."

"I know, I just…I don't know. I guess I have to get used to us being different now."

"Pam, the only thing different is that I'm independent again, I've gotten my life back, and want you to be part of it. Why is that hard for you? I can work all day, go for a beer, and it doesn't mean anything. It's what people all over the world do. I would have picked you up and we could have gone together, if I'd thought you'd have come."

What he was saying made perfect sense—so why was she still apprehensive? Had she been treating him like one of the residents without realizing it? The people who stayed at the shelter were strictly forbidden to drink, but those rules didn't apply to Ted anymore; it had been a knee-jerk reaction on her part, but what did that say about her?

Was she having problems thinking about him outside of the shelter, as an independent man who loved her? Did she only know how to navigate their relationship when he was defined by the rules of the shelter? Did that make things safe? Did she even know the Ted Ramsey who existed outside? She thought she did, but at the moment, it was all confusing as her mind spun with a thousand new questions.

"I don't know, Ted—I love you, too. I do think of you as my equal, of course I do—but I don't feel right allowing you to take on that kind of burden for me. I can't explain it right, but I can't do it."

He looked incredulous and hurt. She wanted to make it right, but she didn't know how to do that. She couldn't lie to him, but the truth was murky, even to her.

"So you would rather risk losing this place than leaning on me the way I had to lean on you so many times? Let me help, Pam."

"I…I can't. Not like that."

The door that had been opening between them shut again.

Ted shook his head, the pain he was obviously in clear in his voice, though he stood tall, proud. "I miss you like hell. I love you, and I want you so much I ache. Life is empty without you, but dammit, I won't be less than a whole man to you, Pam. I won't go through life that way. So you decide… and if you think you can lean on me, let me love you the way you've loved me, let me be there for you like you are for everyone else, then you call me. I have my pride, too. I'm not going to settle for less than everything from you."

He was out the door before she could respond, not that she knew what to say. Her heart went with him, ripped from her chest and leaving her alone with cold confusion.

Lost, she wrapped her arms around herself. She didn't know what to do—her world was unraveling and she didn't know how to make it stop. Ted was gone, and she was on the verge of losing the shelter, as well. So she did the only thing she could—she sat down and went back to work.

12

RAFE LAY AWAKE, sighing heavily as Joy slept. She'd passed out in his arms after a couple glasses of wine. His body was aching for hers after the torturous hours of sexy teasing. Had he been crazy to suggest the all-day-foreplay idea? *Nah.* They'd enjoyed every minute of it.

Still, their timing might have been a little off. She'd had an emotionally exhausting day, and he was frustrated beyond reason. They'd made some progress. He was getting to know the real Joy, and she'd actually loosened up a little. The idea she had about herself as passionless was crazy, but he also knew there was no way to convince her except by demonstration. If given the opportunity, he would be happy to oblige, but her pleasure was paramount. As turned on as he was, he wasn't about to engage in any more one-sided sex.

If only he could sleep as well, there'd be no problem. He closed his eyes, knowing it was a useless pursuit, and opened them again moments later, looking out the partially opened window into the side yard. He enjoyed having the bed next to the window, as well—it was a luxury that he'd never thought about in the city, where it was too noisy and hot.

Though, as much as he loved holding Joy next to him, there was something about being in bed with a deeply slumbering partner that made his insomnia even more excruciating. It was as if she'd gone somewhere he couldn't follow, which was pretty much true. He'd been left behind, and that added a new layer of stress to being awake. Now he was awake *and* alone.

Sleep was an experience that couples shared as much as anything else, not that he'd ever had a relationship last long enough to know. His job hadn't exactly been a good one for carrying on long-term relationships. He wanted nothing more than to be able to fall asleep right now and wake up tangled with Joy, and then they could pursue other pleasures, rested and relaxed.

She stirred in his arms, breaking his train of thought—thankfully—since thinking too much was the enemy in the middle of the night.

She curled close and planted a sleepy kiss on his chest. One simple touch and he was instantly hard and ready. Great. Now he was awake and turned on.

When she murmured something softly against his skin and moved her hand over him, stroking his length, he groaned her name and nudged her face up toward him. Her eyes remained shut. She was smiling, though, and wanton in how she arched against him, sliding her leg over his, bringing his cock in direct contact with her core. He gasped, his body seeking the contact even as his mind knew he should back away.

She was dreaming…and fast asleep.

He placed his hands on her upper arms to try to lever her away. Before she could do what he knew she was about to, he shifted, and she landed on his hip instead.

She was kissing and touching him all over, and he wondered if he should do this—she was asleep.

She dipped her head down and drew the head of his erection into her mouth and sucked, circling him with a velvet sweep of her tongue. He cried out, fisting his hands into the sheets so tightly he heard the elastic snap as they loosened from the edges. She was driving him insane with her mouth.

"Hon, are you awake? Joy?" he said roughly, trying to wake her, but then thought better of it. She was enjoying herself, and she knew she was with him—she was repeating his name with every kiss down the inside of his thigh. She had suggested using her dreams as a means of bridging into real-life sex, so he tried to get more comfortable with the idea. After grabbing a condom off the nighttable and sheathing himself, he lay back, relaxing.

He would let her do whatever she wanted—act out her dream, her fantasy, and play it by ear. If she stopped, God help him, he would stop, too.

"Do you like this?" she said sexily, brushing the ends of her silky hair over his sex, making him dizzy.

"I love it. I love everything you do," he said truthfully, and it occurred to him that he'd rarely been the passive recipient of lovemaking in his life. He was used to taking a more active role, setting the pace.

It was different—and nice—having her take the lead. He also suspected in real life she wouldn't be as bold or as aggressive. He swallowed hard as she ran a finger lightly over his sac.

When she looked up again, her face was illuminated by desire and need. She leaned over him slowly, emerging from the dark like a succubus, his lover who only came awake at night. It was incredibly sexy how she moved so sensuously, and for a moment he questioned if it was her dream or his. Even though sleeping, she was intriguingly accurate in her movements as she touched him everywhere and then gently drew her hand over his eyes.

"No looking…just feel," she commanded in a husky whisper, at once sounding like the daytime Joy he knew, but also not like her at all. He couldn't repress the erotic thrill of his sight being denied. She slid down his body, straddling him. He literally held his breath as he waited for what she'd do next, hoping.

She didn't take him right away, but moved along his shaft, riding the length of him without penetrating, her nipples grazing his chest as her moans became more and more excited—as did he.

Finally, when he thought he might lose it if she kept on, she enveloped him in one deep, downward thrust. She rode him hard, her palms planted solidly on his chest as she took what she wanted and gave so much in return. He'd been waiting so long to be with her like this that he tried to slow down, to make it last, but she was driving him over the edge with her.

He hung on, unsure how much longer he could last. The hard spasms wringing his cock told him in no uncertain terms that she was coming—and he let go and drove up inside. His orgasm triggered another one for her, much to his delight. She collapsed against him as he pulsed inside of her, enjoying the vestiges of his own climax.

"Joy?"

"Mmm. That was nice," she said sleepily against his chest, cuddling in. As far as he could tell, she hadn't woken up at all.

JOY STRETCHED OUT IN BED, more rested and satisfied than she had been in a long while. A glance at the clock told her it wasn't morning, yet she was alert and awake. However, something felt off—sitting up, she looked around, disoriented. She was completely nude for one, but that wasn't what was bothering her.

Rafe had come to bed with her, and now he was gone.

Grabbing her robe from the chair, she wondered if he'd left. She'd had another dream—a fantastic dream. The memory of it was wonderful, though she wished yet again that she could tap into that kind of passion when she was awake—it was obvious she was capable of it, so what was the problem?

As she hurried down the hallway, she stopped midstride, noting a particularly pleasant soreness between her legs. Her muscles were loose and relaxed, as they might be after a good workout. Something was definitely different.

She'd dreamed about Rafe, but she suspected she hadn't been completely dreaming. At least that wasn't what her body was telling her.

Entering the kitchen, she saw the back door open—she never left her door open like that.

"Rafe?"

"Out here," he responded in a quiet voice, and she stepped outside, tugging the robe more tightly.

"What are you doing?"

He was sitting on the swing on her backyard deck, quiet in the dark of the early morning.

"I couldn't sleep. I needed to get up, get some air. Sometimes when I'm laying awake for too long, it's like the dark is closing in on me. I have to get out."

"I understand, I just wondered where you went."

"Nice to be missed."

She heard the smile in his voice and went over to join him on the swing. "It must be close to morning."

"Another hour or so before sunrise, I'd say."

"Rafe..."

"Hmm?"

"Did we... I mean, did I...uh...?"

"Yes. You did. We did. Do you remember?"

"I remember the dream. My body remembers the real part, if you know what I mean. I can feel the, uh, after effects."

"Are you okay with that?" He turned to her, sounding curious.

She thought for a moment, then nodded. "I'm glad.... In my dream, I, uh..."

"Took control, rode me like the wild hussy you obviously are," he teased and she thumped him playfully in the arm.

"Smart guy. I guess I did that for real?"

"You sure did. It was awesome."

She was ridiculously pleased at his words, and relaxed. "It's a little weird, to think I could act it out so precisely, but I don't remember, not really. It's like a, well, like a dream."

"Do you remember how you got on top of me, and drove me to the edge? Do you remember coming...twice? I love how your face looks when you let go—you're beautiful anyway, but right in that moment, it's awesome," he said reverently.

Her face flamed. She did remember, though she wasn't used to the intimate flattery, and hadn't expected it.

"I do remember. I didn't know I'd actually done it—I'm not usually that forward."

"You can be that forward with me anytime you want, Joy. It was incredible."

"You still couldn't sleep."

"No, the two things aren't related. Lack of sex wasn't ever the reason I couldn't sleep," he said, and then, as if realizing how he'd sounded, tried to backtrack, but she put a finger to his lips, smiling. She had no doubt that Rafe had had lovers whenever he'd wanted them, but for some reason it didn't matter—he was here with her, now.

"I mean, uh, in other words, lack of sleep killed my sex life, not the other way around. I think it all stems from stress caused by my burnout."

She rushed to reassure him, not wanting to lose the mood. "No, I know what you mean. Don't worry."

His hand snaked around the back of her neck, drawing her in for a kiss that quickly turned hot. Caught up in the kiss, she gasped when his hand was suddenly under the flap of the robe, caressing her nipple into immediate hardness, and desire flooded her.

"Rafe, my goodness, we're in my backyard," she protested on a half laugh, half sigh, but he kissed her again, and she put her hand against the front of his jeans—he was as hard as a rock, and she moaned in pleasure at the discovery.

"I know."

"Would you like to go back inside?"

"Why don't we just stay here?"

"Out here? On the deck?"

"Sure. Why not? It's cool and dark, and I think that your dream life is telling you to be more aggressive, more adventurous, Joy. Find your passions, and run with them. Let go. As great as it was earlier, I'd like to share that with you when we're both awake. What do you think?"

She bit her lip, looking around—Warren's house was empty, obviously, and the next house was a full yard away, and her trees and hedges provided some privacy. No lights were on; the street was silent—they were completely alone.

"Okay." She took the plunge, her heart racing as she undid her robe, opening it, though not taking it off. It was enough exposure, more than she would have ever indulged in before. The idea of what they were about to do sent shivers of anticipation down her spine.

"Oh—wait, no protection," he said.

As he started to get up, she placed a hand on his arm. "I'm protected. I've taken the pill for years, and I'm okay, you know, health wise," she said, knowing that she didn't want him to leave her right now unless there was very good reason, since she might lose her nerve.

"Aw, babe, I'm good with that. The thought of being inside of you with nothing between us is a dream come true," he said roughly, releasing the snap on his jeans, and she wasted no time diving her hand inside, stroking him gently.

"You always feel so good, Rafe. I love touching you," she whispered, telling him she was as turned on as he was. She was, completely and utterly turned on. Rafe was right—she did have passion, particularly for him.

"You drive me crazy...the way you put your mouth on me earlier, then took control, I loved it," he responded and a thrill of excitement ran through her.

"You liked me taking control?"

He looked her in the eyes, utterly serious. "I loved it. I love watching you do me, sliding over me, touching me everywhere.... I'm yours for the taking, babe. Anything you want, I'll give it to you," he said, sliding his hand down between her legs and rubbing his thumb over her clit until she was shaking with need.

"Rafe, sit.... Sit back on the swing," she said in a trembling voice, aroused beyond all measure. The cool morning air played over her hot skin, and she watched as he did exactly as she said, pushing his jeans down his long legs to the floor of the deck and sitting back on the swing, watching her, but not moving a muscle.

"Want to sit on Santa's lap?" His mischievous tone sparked something playful and naughty inside of her, and she laughed, feeling like the sexy woman she was in her dreams.

"I do. I know exactly what I want for Christmas."

"Come on over and tell me."

"I'd rather show you," she said seductively, poising herself before him as if to sit, raising the bottom of her robe and lowering down, taking him in deep, until the base of his erection pushed against her pubic bone. She snuggled her backside against his lap, finding her balance, and leaned back on him.

"That's perfect. You fit against me, around me, so absolutely perfectly," he said, his voice ragged, and she knew he was as aroused as she was. His arms came around her, holding her in place as he pushed the swing in motion, the sway creating a gentle rocking motion without either of them actually moving.

"Is this what you wanted?" he asked, his voice thick with excitement.

"Yes," she gasped, winding her hands up around the back of his neck, holding on, kissing his jawline. He kept her still, and didn't thrust or urge her to move, the swing levering them against each other, his shaft buried so deeply inside her she embraced every inch of him and yet wanted more.

"What about this?" he asked, sliding one hand down between her legs as he parted the slick flesh there to rub his long fingers over all the right spots.

"Oh, yes...especially that," she agreed. The swing's movement deepened the motion, and she began to tighten unbearably.

Rafe gave up the Santa game, his face against the back of her neck where he investigated the taste of her skin quite thoroughly. She closed her eyes, the swing moving them together like a single, undulating wave.

The swaying motion was so slow, so deep, and she was hypnotized by the onslaught of sensations that she had no control over. Groaning in ecstasy as he uttered guttural, raw words in her ear, she gave herself up and was lifted out of herself, the world around her, traveling to some special, magical place with Rafe.

He filled her so completely, she wasn't sure she could breathe. Her core was hot and slick, the friction unbearable, and she needed to find relief, though the thought of stopping was also unbearable.

At precisely the right moment, he tipped his hips up from the seat of the swing, ever so slightly, thrusting deeper and catapulting her over the edge. The powerful climax took her so thoroughly by surprise that she cried out, regardless of their semi-public location.

His lips caught her exclamations, swallowed them with his own groans of satisfaction as he pulsed inside of her. She knew she'd never experienced anything quite so miraculous as they drifted down from the heights together, wrapped around each other as intimately as two people could be.

They sat together, still swinging gently back and forth, and she knew something had changed for her. Something deep, something more than desire or even gratitude tugged at her. She didn't want to think. She hated to even get up and have to separate from him at all.

Still, as she opened her eyes, flashing lights against the trees and Warren's roof caught her eye.

"Those Christmas lights look funny," she commented.

Rafe jerked upright, keeping his arms around her as he stood, stabilizing her so she wouldn't fall.

"Shit—those aren't lights—it's a fire."

13

JOY RAN INSIDE. Frantically searching for her cell phone, she found it on the counter and dialed 911. Rafe had taken off like a shot, clad only in jeans and bare feet, yelling after her to call for help as he bolted across the street to the house that was burning. She'd called after him—what did he plan to do? Her hands shook as she reported the fire and raced around the house grabbing her clothes, anxious to go find Rafe.

She knew the house belonged to the older lady he always talked with, Bessie, whose lights he'd helped string. The elderly widow whose lights Joy had grumped and groused about, and whom she'd refused to help when Rafe had asked her the week before.

She hung up—she didn't exactly have time to indulge in guilt—and ran back into the street. Sirens screamed in the distance, and the neighbors emerging from their homes were milling about in various states of morning dress, but she didn't see Rafe. Where was he?

She watched the flames engulf the house, black

smoke pouring out of the windows, and knew in her heart where he was. He'd gone in. That was why he'd run off so quickly—Rafe had gone inside to try to save Bessie. She felt utterly helpless, and sick with worry.

Finally, fire engines and a rescue unit ripped up the small street, an ambulance on their heels, pulling to a quick halt in the front yard. The outside air was acrid and thick as the sun rose in a halo of smoke over the house. Joy was hit by the intense heat when she ran up to the firefighter closest to her and grabbed his arm, shouting to him that Rafe had gone inside.

He and three other men dragging heavy hoses headed for the porch as Rafe appeared in the door, an archway of fire framing them all. Joy held her breath as two of the firefighters took the body of the small woman from Rafe's arms, and another helped Rafe away from the house as his body clutched in a fit of choking coughs.

All of a sudden, the arch over the front porch collapsed, Christmas lights and all, right where Rafe and the other men had stood moments before. Police arrived, and they corralled people back to the other side of the street, but Joy stayed in place, all the action happening around her as if she'd become invisible. No one bothered her, or she didn't notice.

She couldn't see Rafe at all, and that snapped her back to life. She rushed forward to where she'd spotted him last. The sounds of flames, rushing water, loud engines and louder shouts surrounded her, but she had only one focus: Rafe. A fireman blocked her path and she pushed past him.

"You have to let me by. My, uh… My husband is hurt—he went in the house." She shook his arm, making him listen. "He's the guy with no shirt—I saw him come out, but I can't find him—I have to make sure he's okay. Please," she pleaded desperately.

The fireman nodded. "Your husband saved that woman's life, ma'am. He's over there." He pointed her in the direction of a rescue vehicle where Rafe sat on the edge between the open doors, an EMT handing him an oxygen mask. She took a few steps and stumbled, tears blurring her vision.

"Rafe, oh, my God," she cried, throwing her arms around him. "What on earth…I didn't think you were going to go *in* there when you ran off," she said, holding on tight.

His chest rumbled against her, and she didn't know if he was coughing or laughing, but he squeezed her tightly and then gently disengaged her arms from his neck, waving away the EMT who was hovering.

"I'm fine—I knew the house since I'd been in there a few times, and I found her easily. Just sucked up some smoke is all. It was only a minute or two I was in there, no big deal."

He coughed again, and she drew back, looking

into his face, something powerful arcing between them. This was more than a two-week fling. She knew it, deep inside her heart.

He caressed her cheek. His tone had been reassuring, as it must have been for hundreds of people before her, people he reassured and saved every day. Suddenly she didn't want to be the one being protected—or rather, she didn't mind his concern, but he was the one who needed the help right now. Why hadn't she seen it before?

"I'm okay, Joy. Not even a scratch, see?"

"It could have been a lot more than a scratch."

"But it wasn't. Bessie's okay, and I'm okay."

The image of his handsome, soot-stained face was engraved into her memory, and her heart, and she couldn't find words, so she simply held on to him a little longer. When his arms slipped around her, too, hugging her close, in spite of herself she fell in love with him right there on the spot.

Too bad he would be out of her life in a little over a week. He planned to head back to New York right after New Year's.

She loved Rafe, but he was leaving. What had passed between them a moment ago was something stronger than lust, but did he love her, too?

Rafe's gaze followed the movements of the people around him, the firefighters getting control of the blaze, the onlookers talking among themselves, the police keeping people back. The ambu-

lance roared past them, whisking Bessie away—
whose life Rafe had definitely saved.

Joy could see how much it all meant to him, and
how painful it was for him to be on the outside
looking in. Rafe was about helping people; that was
who he was. He saved lives; things like running
into burning buildings came as naturally to him as
breathing came to everyone else. Somehow, he'd
even managed to break down the walls Joy had built
around herself and help her, too.

She'd never been more sure of herself in her life
than she was right at that moment—more alive,
more in love—and it was about more than sex. Who
was helping Rafe? She was immediately ashamed,
her life and her problems having been the center of
their focus to this point. Whether he loved her or
not, she knew what she had to do. This time, it was
about Rafe.

Everything crystallized; all the concerns she'd
had, all the neuroses, pressures and worries that
had plagued her life fell away, meaningless. She'd
spent her life withholding the best of herself, afraid
to give in case someone should take what she was
offering and walk away. Ever since her mother had
left, she'd held the most vulnerable parts of herself
back, determined never to let anyone else hurt her
that much again.

With everyone except for Rafe. Maybe it was different for him because he was the opposite. He opened

himself to life and he wasn't afraid of anything. He did what he did because it mattered to him.

What mattered to her?

Certainly not the toy company, their profit margins or the promotion she'd been so determined to get. None of that mattered.

There was the shelter. That mattered. Maybe she'd been going about everything the wrong way— she wanted her work to make a difference, the way Rafe's did. She wanted to use her talents to help people who needed it, like Pam and the residents at the shelter. She wanted to throw herself out into the world and see what happened, and if she got hurt, well, there were worse things. Like the numbed life she had been living.

There was more than enough help to go around for clients who could afford to pay for it, but what about everyone else? While financial security had always meant a lot to her, she could see it wasn't the cornerstone of life, nor should it be.

Her dreams of Rafe had been pushing her to risk, to take more chances, to go after what she wanted and to make things happen—and not only in bed, but in life.

As the meaning of the moment dawned on her, it was as if a latch opened up inside of her and she could breathe freely for the first time in her life. There wouldn't be any more dreams, no more talking and acting out in her sleep. She slanted a gaze at Rafe's sweaty, dirty, lovely chest and smiled—she'd be plenty able to live out her fantasies wide awake from now on. All of them.

Boldly taking his hand as they crossed the street back to her house, she knew she wanted to start her new lease on life by helping him as much as he'd helped her.

The question was how?

RAFE WALKED ALONG the hospital hallways, following Joy, who knew her way around the place better than he did, though in his experience all hospitals more or less looked the same.

Garland and fake Christmas trees, menorahs and other holiday items were scattered throughout the stark yellow-white hallway. As much as the decorations aimed to offer holiday cheer, for many of the people in here, and many of their loved ones, it was not a happy season, and no amount of decorations would make it one.

It had often been difficult to get through the holidays when he'd been riding the ambulance—the holidays were a time of year when people could be at their best, or their worst. Loneliness and hardship, poverty and loss were often highlighted, the contrast sometimes too much to bear. Rafe had usually turned to his family to remember what was good and happy about this time of year.

As for right now, two days until Christmas, being

in the hospital reminded him of the sadness he'd had close personal contact with over the years, though there were happy stories, too. The Christmas babies born, the lives saved, the tragedies averted, as was the case with Bessie, whom they'd come to see. Focusing on the upside was how he'd gotten by as long as he had, though apparently he'd lost that ability somewhere along the way.

He'd rarely seen people after he'd brought them to the hospital, and even though he hadn't acted in an official capacity with Bessie, he felt off balance. He held a bunch of flowers in one arm and clasped Joy's hand in his other. She was walking at a slightly faster pace, looking for the room, full of cheer.

To be honest, he'd been surprised when she'd told him she wanted to go with him to the hospital. He'd had the impression that she didn't connect much with her neighbors, but then, a lot of things seemed to have changed with Joy. In the two days since the fire, she'd been far more energized, unbelievably sexy. In bed—and out of it—she was rocking his world.

She was also busy, working on something every minute, usually associated with the shelter. They'd both spent every free minute getting the fundraising party planned, which was why they were late to see Bessie. Christmas was two days away, and Rafe knew how much keeping that shelter open meant to Joy. Still, the changes in her demeanor since the fire were considerable, if a little mysterious to him.

Among other things, she'd taken to wearing her hair down instead of tied back, and she seemed more relaxed. He found it hard to believe that getting over her sexual inhibition had led to such a personality shift, but it didn't really matter. What did matter was that she was happy. He liked to think he had something to do with it.

The more time he spent with Joy, the less he thought about going back to New York, and maybe not even going back to his job. Working hospital shifts and driving ambulance was tough on relationships, and he'd made his work the center of his life for so long because nothing else more important had presented itself. Joy was changing all of that.

As they reached the end of the long hallway, nurses and activity buzzing around, he teetered on the edge of a huge decision. He was technically on a leave of absence, but he was considering making that leave permanent. In fact, maybe he'd already made the choice.

He wanted more time here in San Diego and Joy was the reason for that. Going back to New York without her was quickly becoming a nonoption, but he wasn't sure what she would think about that. Would she want to tie herself down to a relationship with him, when he had no idea what was next?

Stopping by the door of Bessie's room, he heard

voices, and knocked softly, making sure it was okay to enter.

"Rafe! My hero, you come in here," Bessie exclaimed, holding her arms out. She wasn't alone, he could see, a younger, well-dressed couple were sitting at her bedside.

As he hugged Bessie and stood back, he handed her the flowers, aware of Joy right behind him. Reaching back for her hand, he drew her next to him.

"Hey, Bessie. You're looking chipper—glad to see it."

"Yes, well, thanks to you, I'm around here to tell the tale," she said, her eyes moving to Joy. "I see you brought a friend."

"You know Joy, Bessie, from across the street. She called 911 when we saw the fire that morning," he explained and nudged Joy forward.

"Well, I can't thank you enough for that, Joy," Bessie said, her eyes tearing up. "You both saved my life, and the firemen got there in time to at least save many of the things on the second floor—there's smoke damage, but so many of my memories, my wedding pictures, my husband's things, were upstairs," she said, choking up, and couldn't continue.

Joy bent over and hugged Bessie, reassuring her.

"I'd be happy to help get them out and clean things up, if you'd like me to do that. I wish we could have seen it sooner, is all, but Rafe is the real hero. I only made a phone call," Joy said, releasing Bessie from the hug.

She wiped away a few tears and nodded. "They told me as much, and I can't believe you came into that burning building for me," Bessie scolded Rafe gently in an emotional voice, and Rafe stayed silent, not knowing what to say.

"I can see you don't like being told you're a hero, but you are. Anyway, this is my son Charles, and his wife, Melinda. They came as soon as they heard, and I guess I'll be staying with them for a while until the house can be taken care of."

"So you'll be rebuilding?" Joy asked politely, and Bessie nodded.

"The old place needed a lot of repair—it was an overheated circuit that started the fire. I left a Crock-Pot on all night, and I guess the fire started in the wall where it was plugged in, so they say."

"That's awful, Bessie, but at least you're okay," Rafe added, shaking hands with Charles and Melinda, who looked both relieved and concerned as they chatted. Rafe didn't want to intrude on the family moment—he was used to being on the outside of such things.

"We'd love for Mother to come live with us permanently, but she likes being on her own. It's nice to know she has such good neighbors," Charles said.

"There aren't many who would run into a

burning building to save someone," Bessie added with blatant admiration.

"What do you do for a living, Rafe? Mom said you were here on vacation?" Bessie's daughter-in-law asked.

"I'm a paramedic, back in New York," Rafe said casually and tried to change the conversation to focus back on Bessie, but his attempt failed yet again.

"Well, you're a hero to us—I hope you'll let us do something to show our appreciation," Melinda said, and Rafe waved away her offer.

"That's not necessary, really."

"We insist. Please." Charles met his gaze, and Rafe knew it was important to the younger man to do something to show his gratitude, but Rafe wasn't about to accept any personal payment for doing what anyone could have done.

"I'll tell you what. If you're all in town, there's a Christmas fund-raiser at a local homeless shelter tomorrow night that we're helping out. We'd love it if you could come, Charles and Melinda, and Bessie, if you're up to it."

"We're probably taking Mother home tomorrow morning, but we would like to make a donation. I wish we could do more," Charles said. "You saved my mother. After having lost Dad, this could have been the saddest holiday ever for our family, and you changed that. We can't express what that means to us. Thank you."

Rafe nodded, accepting the thanks awkwardly. Joy's hand was on his back as they all shook hands and said their goodbyes. Walking down the hall, Joy turned to him as they waited for the elevator.

"Rafe, in all the years you did your job, did anyone ever say thank you?"

He shrugged. "Sure. Some people sent cookies, or dropped a note."

"No one ever personally thanked you for helping them?"

"New York is a big place, Joy, and we handled so many cases every day…. There were several ambulance companies, even more drivers. It was a daunting number of people. Patients couldn't tell us apart let alone know our names, especially when they're in crisis. It was our job to help them. Thanks isn't necessary," he explained.

The elevator doors opened, and as she stepped inside, she raised her emotion-filled eyes to his.

"It's something you deserve."

"Knowing we've helped is enough."

Or was it? he asked himself, though somewhat ashamed of the question. What he did wasn't supposed to be about recognition, but had the endless stream of people whom they'd helped and never seen again finally gotten to him? Was it the source of his burnout and insomnia?

Rafe didn't like that idea. Maybe it was more about never knowing how most of those patients ended up—he only saw them at their worst, but never, as he'd had the chance to do with Bessie, when things turned for the better.

In the shelter, Joy and Pam could see someone move from destitution to success, from being dependent to self-sufficient, and that was a reward he'd never had. All he'd seen was the never-ending moments of crisis. It was a reality he'd never acknowledged before.

Joy murmured her agreement with what he'd said, but Rafe kept his other thoughts to himself, considering them less than noble. Having Joy think anything less of him bothered him a lot. Still, did he always have to be the hero? Was his ego so bound up in what he did that he didn't even realize it? He didn't like to think so, but maybe.

As they left the hospital, Joy was distracted, lost in thought, even through lunch.

"You're quiet," he observed, toying with his own food and caught up in his own thoughts. It was nice that they could be quiet together, but he wondered what was on her mind.

"Sorry, going over party stuff. Thinking about Bessie, and how happy I am about how it all turned out—I hope the same happens for Pam."

"It was good of your boss to give you these few days off before the holiday."

"Uh, yes—" she looked down at her soup "—I

told him about the fire and everything, and he was very supportive."

"So things are working out there," he prompted, picking up on some weird sense that she was holding something back from him.

"Yeah, things are working out very well, but really, the shelter is what I am focusing on right now. That's where my real passion lies, and I guess I never realized that."

"That's wonderful, Joy—they're lucky to have you."

His thoughts circled back to his own situation. Maybe getting his old sense of purpose back wasn't the right move—maybe it was time to try something new. Instead of trying to find the meaning his life used to have, he should look for something new, much as Joy was discovering. He'd always assumed he'd drive ambulances forever, but now he was questioning that. The prospect of returning to the job brought him none of the anticipation and excitement it used to. That was something he had to accept. It was over.

When they returned home, Joy headed off to run some errands for the shelter party, and Rafe sat by the phone for a long time. Finally, convinced he was doing the right thing, he picked it up and dialed his boss. It was time to leave his old life behind him.

14

"IT'S CRAZY—I CAN'T believe all these people showed up! This is miraculous!" Pam swirled around to face Joy, nearly dropping her punch on the person next to her, more thrilled and happy than she had been in weeks. The party was packed; music was playing; residents were decked out in their Christmas best and making contacts and showing the employers, supporters and community members who had come to the party that they were good, decent people who deserved a second chance. It was all she could have dreamed of and more.

Still, her cheer lapsed slightly as she noticed one gap in the crowd; Ted hadn't come. She hadn't been sure if he would or not. She'd left an invitation on his phone, but he'd never responded. She'd been too busy to brood on everything that had happened between them. One thing for certain—she knew she still didn't want him taking financial responsibility for the shelter. Not because she didn't think he could handle it, but because, well…this place was *hers*. She didn't want to have the burden placed on anyone else but her.

However, at least for the moment, it looked as if they were becoming financially secure again. Donations were pouring in faster than they had in a long while, and she'd already set up several new contacts for services. She thought this Christmas party would be an annual event—thank God for Joy.

"You really saved us here, Joy. I know the social and counseling aspects of this business inside out, but I guess I was never a great publicist—I never really thought about bringing the community inside, opening the doors and letting them see the place, who lives here, how we work," she said, giving her friend's hand a squeeze.

"I'm so happy for you, Pam, that this is going so well. The shelter is going to benefit big time, in spite of the rumors—no one is talking about it, or even cares. It's so obvious you do good work here, and that the place is an asset to the community."

"Thanks—it's more than I ever dreamed of. Thanks to you and your help—you are a PR goddess. Speaking of which, what about your promotion at Carr? Have you heard anything?"

"I actually…I called Ken today and turned it down—in fact, I quit."

Pam was obviously shocked.

"You quit? Your job?"

"Yes. The corporate life isn't for me. Never was. I worked hard and I was good at it, but I was never happy. Not really. One side benefit is I saved and invested a good bit of money. Now I can afford time off to find out what I really love doing, and I have a feeling it's going to be finding some career through which I can help support organizations like yours."

"That's fantastic! That's such a huge step, Joy."

"It's wonderful. It was time for me to make a move."

"You do seem like a load has been taken off, though. You seem happier. Lighter."

"There is some other news, though. I need you to keep it between us."

Pam leaned in, noting how Joy's gaze had traveled over to Rafe, and she wondered if her friend was about to share wedding plans.

"I may be moving to New York."

"What?" Pam said loudly, drawing the attention of some people nearby. "What? Why?"

"I quit my job to be with Rafe. I want to help him work through this sleep problem and get back to his job. He loves it, Pam. You should have seen him at that fire, and with Bessie afterward. It's his life. I want to share that life with him, hopefully. So I'm going to tell him later that I want to go back to New York with him when he's finished his vacation here. I'd like to explore new career options for myself, and help him get back on his feet."

"Wow. That's not what I was expecting, but *wow*. That's huge! Are you sure? I mean, it's clear you two are crazy about each other, though—and

I'm happy for you. It's nice to be madly in love, but you know, that's a big chance to take," Pam said, happy for Joy, but unable to keep a wistful note from her voice.

"Well, we haven't actually said anything about love yet—in fact, we haven't said anything about anything, but it's time—I'm crazy about him. I have to take a chance. There's just something…"

"Special. I think you're right. There is. You should do whatever's necessary to hold on to it."

Joy hugged her. "Pam, thanks. I know you mean that. I know it's especially difficult because things have been rough between you and Ted lately, but—"

"No, please. Not tonight. It's killing me what's happened with us, but I think it's over. I haven't heard from him since our blowout the other night, and he's not here now, so, you know. I think that's it," she said, trying to sound brave, but her voice quavered, giving her raw emotions away.

"I don't think so. Honey, I know you love Ted like crazy, and he loves you, too—but you both let your pride get in the way. Rafe has taught me that relationships are about helping each other, leaning on each other, and maybe you might have a teensy bit of a hard time doing that with Ted?"

Pam started to bristle, but then gave in, her shoulders slumping. "Maybe. I guess it's because I'm used to standing on my own."

"You're the heart of this place, Pam, no doubt,

but you can't be afraid to lean on the people who want to help you."

"I know. I guess in my heart I didn't want this place to fail, and I didn't want anyone—including Ted, especially Ted—to think I'd failed, as well. When he wanted to take on the loan, I wasn't protecting him, I was protecting *me*. I wanted to save the place on my own terms."

"You did."

"No, I did it with help from my friends—and I should have let Ted help, too."

"It's never too late."

"It may well be. I don't know how to make Ted understand. I really hurt him."

Joy smiled, her gaze sliding to the door. "Actually, I think you're in for a surprise."

Pam followed Joy's gaze. There was Ted standing tentatively by the door, a group of people around him as they all dealt with their coats and said hellos. The world dropped away as Pam's eyes met his and she started breathing again—had it only been a few days? He looked so handsome, and she knew Joy was right—pride and ego were no reasons to throw away the best thing in her life.

She started to make her way through the crowd, to go to him, but Joy's hand was on her arm.

"Wait. Just a minute."

Pam stopped, puzzled, as Ted and the group he'd apparently come with went forward to the platform at the front of the room. As they did so, Pam realized that she knew the four men who followed along with Ted—though they looked so different now. She held her breath, realizing what was going on and not quite believing it. Ted took the podium, appearing a bit apprehensive as he cleared his throat, using his booming baritone to get the room's attention.

"Hello, everyone, happy holidays. I'm Ted Ramsey, and I used to be a resident here, not so long ago. I was thirty-eight when I lost everything and ended up on the street. I used to live in New Orleans, where I worked as a handyman in the building where I lived. Because of Hurricane Katrina, I lost my home and my job, and the building was never rebuilt. For me, everything was gone. Absolutely everything," he said, clearing his throat again. The room was completely silent, listening, and he continued.

"I was evacuated to San Diego. I didn't have any family, and my friends were all in similar situations, so I lived in alleys, didn't eat or sleep for days in a row sometimes. I tried to find jobs, but I didn't have money for new clothes, no address, and the more you're out there, the less anyone wants to give you a chance. To most people, I was a bum. I was arrested for sleeping in a park and the cop who let me off told me about Second Chance."

Pam put her hands to her mouth, seeing the admiration among the listeners as Ted continued.

"Thing is, anyone can end up homeless—you think it can't happen to you, but it can. The world can take you to some pretty low places. However, because of this shelter and people like Pam, there are second chances. All of us here—" he gestured to the people standing proudly behind him "—found a new life though this place, and some of us found even more than that," he said, his eyes meeting Pam's, his tone husky with emotion. She'd never loved him more. He smiled then, as he wrapped up, and her world lit brighter.

"We're hoping you'll listen to our stories, and support this place well into the future, in any way you can."

Ted stepped down to a deafening level of applause and cheers, the audience turning their attention back to the stage to listen to the other members of the group. Joy hugged Pam, her own eyes teary.

"Ted did this on his own—he told me, but he wanted it to be a surprise. He contacted every person he could find to come back here and share their stories. They flew in from all over. He did it for you, most of all though, Pam, because he loves you. Make no mistake about that," Joy said, and Pam could only nod, emotions bunching any words she might have spoken into a soundless knot in her throat as Joy stepped away.

Then Ted was there, large and handsome, close and warm, and all she could do was throw her arms around him in front of God and everyone without thinking twice. She didn't care what anyone thought, only Ted. She loved him, and she told him so, needing him to know that he'd always come first with her. When his arms wrapped around her and their lips met, Pam knew it was going to be one of the best Christmases ever.

JOY SHRIEKED AS SHE and Rafe ran from the car to her house, lugging bags of gifts and goodies from the party, laughing as they got soaked anyway, not moving nearly fast enough as the rain poured down in dark sheets. The heat wave that had been baking Southern California for weeks was finally giving way as cooler weather settled in for Christmas.

It wasn't snow, but she'd take it.

Dropping the bags safely on her porch, she looked at Rafe—quite the stud, decked out in his suit. Laughing with glee, she ran back down the steps and began dancing out into the yard, arms spread, glorying in the cool wash of the rain.

With a laugh, he joined her and pulled her up against him, taking her mouth in a drugging kiss as the rain poured over them and they swayed back and forth in a slow, wet dance. It thrilled her that Rafe was able to get her so hot, so fast, and most of all it thrilled her that she'd discovered such a deep well of passion in her life, and she wanted to share it with him.

"Want to take the party inside?" she asked seductively, tugging at his tie.

"Absolutely."

Arm in arm they walked back up the porch and in the door, peeling off their wet clothes layer by layer until they were nude and shivering up against each other.

"I think a hot shower is needed," she said, her teeth chattering. She squealed as Rafe picked her up in his arms and climbed the stairs. In the shower, he returned to kissing her, turning the hot water on high without breaking their lip-lock even for a second.

Joy was in heaven as the steamy water and Rafe's touch chased away the chill. He was so solid and warm, her hands drifting over every inch of his skin was a pursuit of which she could never tire.

When he hoisted her up, pressing her back against the tile and sliding home, deep inside her welcoming body, it was all so right and natural, as if their bodies were made for each other and no one else. She gave herself up to him, completely trusting, more than happy to follow his lead as he made her body soar with pleasure she hadn't known she was capable of.

Joy hoped she'd get a lot more chances to make up for lost time in the physical-pleasure department, but what she was experiencing with Rafe was also deepened by emotions she'd never felt for any other man.

Coming down from their interlude, they soaped each other from head to toe and then rubbed each other dry with soft towels. Rafe trotted off to grab some wine and agreed to meet her downstairs. It was late, but what the hell? It was the night before Christmas Eve and she wanted to celebrate.

She couldn't believe she'd quit her job, or how good it felt. She knew it deep inside, in her gut. It was new to be so sure, so confident. She liked it.

She'd have to find something else eventually, but for now she planned on enjoying an extended vacation, hopefully with the man of her dreams. Joy paused, a little riff of nervousness running down her spine as she contemplated what she'd say. What if Rafe was still in favor of their original plan? A few weeks of no-strings fun that she now very much wanted to attach some very hefty strings to?

Donning a sheer nightgown, Joy found him on the sofa where he sat quietly, lounging only in a pair of flannel house pants, his beautiful chest bare, and her heart fluttered at the picture he made. The rain poured outside, and he didn't seem to notice her arrival as he studied the twinkling lights of the Christmas tree with an intense expression that didn't seem to fit with their lighthearted evening.

"You're staring a hole in that tree—everything okay?"

He looked up, smiling. "Fine. Just thinking. The tree is pretty. I notice you snuck some gifts underneath."

She sat down close by his side, cuddling in. "A few."

"I have some things for you, too, though I have to wrap them," he confessed.

She swatted him playfully—they'd said no gifts, but now that she was in full swing with the Christmas spirit, she couldn't resist putting some prettily wrapped packages under the tree. Working up her courage, she stood up.

"I have one thing I want to give you now, actually."

He smiled flirtatiously at her. "Again?"

"Not that, at least, not this minute. A real present."

"You don't have to do that, Joy," he said. "We should wait until Christmas morning. It's only one more day."

"I really want to. I really want you to have this now, because I have some things I want to tell you, and it's all wrapped up, so to speak."

"Well, okay. I'm never one to turn down a present," he teased as she walked to her desk on the other side of the room and took a folder from under the large calendar that rested under her computer.

She sat, placing the folder between them, and explained in a rush, "It's not a gift like the ones under the tree, but it's something I wanted you to have for Christmas. I got the idea from Ted, you know, how he contacted all those people for Pam and the shelter, and from our visit to Bessie the other day. I thought, I don't know…that it could help you get over your burnout problem. Just open it and stop me from continuing to babble, okay?"

Rafe looked at her quizzically and slowly reached to open the folder, then pulled out a thick pile of e-mails.

"What is this?"

"Your boss helped me get in touch with some of the people you've helped. When I called them, they were so enthusiastic to finally have a chance to contact you and say thank-you—like you said, at the time someone is picked up, they don't know who you are, and time passes—but so many people jumped at the chance to tell you what your help meant, Rafe. I wanted you to know, too."

He waded through the stack, smiling at some, re-membering others very clearly, caught up in a string of memories that he shared with her as they went through the e-mails together, and when they'd reached the last one, he looked at her, his heart in his eyes.

"Joy…I don't know what to say." He lifted his hand to her face, his expression solemn and emo-tional. "Thank you. This…this is beyond words."

"I did the legwork, but you've done these won-derful things for all of these people, and you've made a huge difference in my world, too, Rafe. I need you to know that. In fact—" She took a deep breath, started to speak, but then stopped.

Her hands were shaking as she knew she teetered on the edge of something wonderful or potentially terrible in her life. What if she was jumping the gun? What if her instincts were off and he didn't want her as much as she hoped he did? Telling Rafe her true feelings, what she wanted, was an enormous risk. The words clogged in her throat. Was she ready? She'd quit her job, turned down a promotion and was determined to start a new life. Only this time, it wasn't her job, but her heart that was on the line.

Rafe looked deeply concerned, as he always did when something troubled her.

"Hey, what can be so horrible? You can tell me anything, Joy."

He took her hands, cold from nerves, and warmed them in his own. She stared for several long moments into his face, the blinking lights of the tree creating a cheerful backdrop that bolstered her courage. It was Christmas, after all. The time for miracles, right?

She took another deep breath, getting the rest of it out as quickly as she could. "How you saved Bessie, and those e-mails, talking to the people you've helped—what you do is so important, so meaningful. I want to have that meaning in life, too, work I can be as passionate about as you are about yours."

"That's wonderful, Joy," he said sincerely. She

knew he meant it, but he also looked guarded and drew back from her slightly. Fear lodged in her chest, but she pushed herself forward. She had to tell him, for better or worse.

"So…I quit my job. I'm not going back to Carr. I love you, Rafe. I love how you make me feel, how you care for others, and how terrific and brave you are. I want to go to New York with you and help you get back to your job. We can work it out together. I want…I bought a…ticket, already," she finished lamely, gripping his fingers tightly because he hadn't let go and she needed something, anything, to hold on to.

"You bought a ticket? To New York?"

She nodded, not particularly encouraged by his incredulous tone.

"You quit your job?"

She nodded again, wishing he would stop repeating everything she'd said, as if she weren't skittish enough already about laying her heart on the line.

"Um, well, okay. I don't know if you'll need that ticket, but—"

Her heart sank and she pulled her hands away quickly. "It's okay, I know, I dumped all of that on you out of nowhere, and if you don't want me to go back with you, I won't. God, I'm such an idiot, I don't know what I was thinking—"

"Joy. Stop," he said softly as he pushed her still-damp hair back from her forehead.

"Huh?"

"Let me finish." He blew out a breath, relief evident in his expression. "For a moment there, I thought you were going to tell me it was over, and I needed to hit the highway. Good thing you didn't, because I love you, too. Utterly and completely."

Confusion stopped her cold. "You love me? You thought I was going to break it off? I don't get it—you said I don't need the ticket...."

"Right. You don't. Because I quit my job, too. I thought I'd stay here in California. Be with you. To start a new life."

Nothing he said could have surprised her more. She sat back, stunned.

"You...You quit? I thought your job meant everything to you. The letters..."

He looked down at the sheaf of papers. "They're fantastic—I'll always treasure them. They're also a goodbye of sorts, I guess."

To say she was stunned was an understatement. "No, Rafe, you can't give up! We can go back to New York—you can be with your family, we'll solve this insomnia problem, and we'll get you back on the ambulance."

"I'm not giving up, I'm letting go. There's a difference."

"Rafe, but," she started to argue, and he held up a hand to stop her.

"The longer I stayed here, the more I was with

you, and away from work, the more I realized I didn't want to go back. It's time for a new phase. A change. I guess I knew that, it was why I got so burned out in the first place, but I wasn't able to accept it until now. I'll find a job here, maybe something new, I don't know yet. Maybe I'll go back to school. Are you willing to take that risk with me? To jump into the future, not knowing what it holds for us?"

"I think…yes…I'd like that," she said, still processing the turn of events.

"I'd love for you to come back and see my city and meet my family, but here you have the shelter, friends, and a life, and I'm getting used to this climate. I want to meet your family, and I think I'd like to try surfing," he finished with a grin.

She stared at him as if he were speaking a language she didn't understand, and he tried to make his case a little more clearly.

"We have time—we can decide what we want, where we want to go, what we want to do, together. There's no rush. I will, however, need a place to live. I was kind of hoping I could move my things in over here." He ended his sentence on a big yawn and shook his head as if to clear it, bringing both of her hands to his lips.

She took a few minutes to absorb what he was telling her—he'd quit his job to stay here, and she'd quit hers to go with him.

It was perfect. They had their whole lives before

them. A real adventure with the man she loved. Her heart raced with excitement at the prospect of her new future, and of sharing it with Rafe.

Finally, she spoke. "I like that idea a lot, you living here. I guess we got each other the same gift," she said, chuckling, leaning her forehead against his.

"Looks like," he said on another yawn, and she looked at him in amazement.

"I can't believe you quit your job for me."

"I'm delighted that you quit your job for me. We have a fresh slate now, a new beginning for both— excuse me," he said, interrupted by a yawn.

"Hey, you're yawning," she observed.

"Uh-huh," he said, rubbing his eyes.

"You look absolutely exhausted."

The import of her words finally dawned on him.

"Joy...I *am* tired—really *tired*," he said in surprise, the sudden need to sleep almost overwhelming.

Whether it was the finality of making a decision about his job, making peace with the past, or having found his place in life with Joy, the tension that had always pulled tight, keeping him awake night after night, seemed to have disappeared. "I guess there's only one way to tell—we have to go to bed."

She stood, holding out her hand to him. "I like that plan. If you're not tired enough to pass out immediately, I bet I can find a few ways to make sure you are," she promised seductively.

He stood and took her hand, pulling her up close, then ran his hand down the length of her back and around the swell of her backside, then back up again. She gloried in his touch, focusing on the hot trail of desire he created, and leaned in for a kiss.

"And to all a good night…."

* * * * *

Kimberley Blackstone didn't notice the waiting horde of media until it was too late. Flashbulbs exploded around her like a New Year's light show. She skidded to a halt, so abruptly her trailing suitcase all but overtook her.

This had to be a case of mistaken identity. Surely. Kimberley hadn't been on the paparazzi hit list for close to a decade, not since she'd estranged herself from her billionaire father and his headline-hungry diamond business.

But no, it was *her* name they called. *Her* face was the focus of a swarm of lenses that circled her like avid hornets. Her heart started to pound with fear-fueled adrenaline.

What did they want?

What was going on?

With a rising sense of bewilderment she scanned the crowd for a clue, and her gaze fastened on a tall, leonine figure forcing his way to the front. A tall, familiar figure. Her head came up in stunned recognition, and their gazes collided across the sea of heads before the cameras erupted with another barrage of flashes, this time right in her exposed face.

Blinded by the flashbulbs—and by the shock of that momentary eye-meet—Kimberley didn't realize his intent until he'd forged his way to her side, possibly by the sheer strength of his personality. She felt his arm wrap around her shoulder, pulling her into the protective shelter of his body, allowing her no time to object. No chance to lift her hands to ward him off.

In the space of a hastily drawn breath, she found herself plastered knee-to-nose against six feet two inches of hard-bodied male.

Ric Perrini.

Her lover for ten torrid weeks, her husband for ten tumultuous days.

Her ex for ten tranquil years.

After all this time, he should not have felt so familiar but, oh dear, he did. She knew the scent of that body and its lean, muscular strength. She knew its heat and its slick power and every response it could draw from hers.

She also recognized the ease with which he'd taken control of the moment and the decisiveness of his deep voice when it rumbled close to her ear. "I have a car waiting outside. Is this your only luggage?"

Kimberley nodded. "I assume you will tell me," she said tightly, "what this welcome party is all about."

"Not while the welcome party is within earshot. No."

Barking a request for the cameramen to stand aside, Perrini took her hand and pulled her into step with his ground-eating stride. Kimberley let him, because he was right, damn his arrogant, Italian-suited hide. Despite the speed with which he whisked her across the airport terminal, she could almost feel the hot breath of the pursuing media on her back.

This was neither the time nor the place for explanations. Inside his car, however, she would get answers.

Now that the initial shock had been blown away— by the haste of their retreat, by the heat of her gathering indignation, by the rush of adrenaline fired by Perrini's presence and the looming verbal battle— her brain was starting to tick over. This had to be her father's doing. And if it was a Howard Blackstone publicity ploy, then it had to be about Blackstone Diamonds, the company that ruled his life.

The knowledge made her chest tighten with a familiar ache of disillusionment.

She'd known her father would be flying in from Sydney for today's opening of the newest in his chain of exclusive, high-end jewelry boutiques. The opulent shopfront sat adjacent to the rival business where Kimberley worked. No coincidence, she thought bitterly, just as it was no coincidence that Ric Perrini was here in Auckland ushering her to his car.

Perrini was Howard Blackstone's right-hand man, second in command at Blackstone Diamonds, a legacy of his short-lived marriage to the boss's daughter. No doubt her father had sent him to fetch her; the question was *why?*

* * * * *

Get swept away down under with the glitz
and glamour of the Blackstone empire as
Kimberley tries to determine the real reason
behind her "reunion" with Ric….

Look for
VOWS & A VENGEFUL GROOM
by Bronwyn Jameson,
in stores January 2008.

When Kimberley Blackstone's father is
presumed dead, Kimberley is required to take
over the helm of Blackstone Diamonds. She
has to work closely with her ex, Ric Perrini, to
battle not only the press, but also the fierce
attraction still sizzling between them. Does Ric
feel the same...or is it the power her share of
Blackstone Diamonds will provide him as he
battles for boardroom supremacy.

Look for

VOWS &
A VENGEFUL GROOM
by

BRONWYN
JAMESON

Available January wherever you buy books

Jachin Black always knew he was an outcast.
Not only was he a vampire, he was a vampire
banished from the Sanguinas society. Jachin, forced
to survive among mortals, is determined to buy
his way back into the clan one day.

Ariel Swanson, debut author of a vampire novel, could
be the ticket he needs to get revenge and take his
rightful place among the Sanguinas again. However,
the unsuspecting mortal woman has no idea of the
dark and sensual path she will be forced to travel.

Look for

RESURRECTION: THE BEGINNING

by

PATRICE MICHELLE

Available January 2008 wherever you buy books.

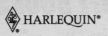

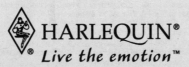

REQUEST YOUR FREE BOOKS!

2 FREE NOVELS PLUS 2 FREE GIFTS!

HARLEQUIN®

Blaze

Red-hot reads!

YES! Please send me 2 FREE Harlequin® Blaze® novels and my 2 FREE gifts. After receiving them, if I don't wish to receive any more books, I can return the shipping statement marked "cancel." If I don't cancel, I will receive 6 brand-new novels every month and be billed just $3.99 per book in the U.S., or $4.47 per book in Canada, plus 25¢ shipping and handling per book and applicable taxes, if any*. That's a savings of at least 15% off the cover price! I understand that accepting the 2 free books and gifts places me under no obligation to buy anything. I can always return a shipment and cancel at any time. Even if I never buy another book from Harlequin, the two free books and gifts are mine to keep forever.

151 HDN EF3W   351 HDN EF3X

Name	(PLEASE PRINT)	
Address		Apt.
City	State/Prov.	Zip/Postal Code

Signature (if under 18, a parent or guardian must sign)

Mail to the **Harlequin Reader Service®**:
IN U.S.A.: P.O. Box 1867, Buffalo, NY 14240-1867
IN CANADA: P.O. Box 609, Fort Erie, Ontario L2A 5X3

Not valid to current Harlequin Blaze subscribers.

Want to try two free books from another line?
Call 1-800-873-8635 or visit www.morefreebooks.com.

* Terms and prices subject to change without notice. NY residents add applicable sales tax. Canadian residents will be charged applicable provincial taxes and GST. This offer is limited to one order per household. All orders subject to approval. Credit or debit balances in a customer's account(s) may be offset by any other outstanding balance owed by or to the customer. Please allow 4 to 6 weeks for delivery.

Your Privacy: Harlequin is committed to protecting your privacy. Our Privacy Policy is available online at www.eHarlequin.com or upon request from the Reader Service. From time to time we make our lists of customers available to reputable firms who may have a product or service of interest to you. If you would prefer we not share your name and address, please check here. ☐

HB07